The Warrior's Call

Dragon Riders of Osnen Book 3

RICHARD FIERCE

Dragonfire Press

Cover design by germancreative.

Cover art by Rosauro Ugang

ISBN: 978-1-947329-30-0

CONTENTS

1

"Something's wrong," Anesko said.

I watched him pace restlessly back and forth across the command tent. He'd called an emergency meeting and asked me to attend, but I didn't know why. The Curates were all present, and between the fire burning in the brazier and the number of people inside the small area, it was stifling. I needed to get some fresh air but not much had been discussed yet.

"I agree," Curate Henrik said. "Where are the others? Why aren't they here yet?"

I glanced at Henrik, then back at Anesko. There was a lot of unease in the camp. So much so that it was almost palpable. Even Maren seemed affected by it. The mysterious creature that was killing dragons was mostly to blame. Whatever it was, it hunted at night and had managed to kill half of the dragons Anesko had brought with him.

"Why did the Conclave approve of this attack if they didn't have a way to combat that spawn of darkness?"

I looked at the woman who had spoken. Her name was Mila. She'd been promoted to Curate as a replacement for Josephine. For the most part, the two were nothing alike. Mila was tall and thin, with blond hair and bright blue eyes. Although she was a noble, she treated everyone with the same dignity. That alone set her apart from all the other nobles I'd encountered.

"Have we received any word from the other schools yet?" Anesko asked.

"No," Henrik confirmed. "And the Conclave hasn't responded to any of the messages we've sent, magical or by bird."

Anesko stopped his pacing and rubbed his hands over his face. It hadn't seemed that long ago since I'd been at the Citadel, yet Anesko had aged a lot since taking over as temporary master. He failed to hide his stress as well as Master Pevus did, but he was doing the best he could. The king's army was at a standstill. Their camp was closer to Midia's border, and the creature had ravaged their forces as well. Rumors were being whispered that the king himself was on his way with reinforcements. I'd asked Maren if that was true, but she had merely shrugged.

"Sir?" I said.

Anesko looked at me.

"Why don't you send a rider to the Conclave? It seems that the messages being sent are either being intercepted or failing to arrive."

"Trust me, Eldwin," Anesko replied. "I would have sent a rider earlier if I thought we could spare one. As it stands, we've taken heavy losses. If that creature attacks our camp, I'd rather have every dragon we can muster to defend against it."

That made sense. All the riders and their dragons had been trained for battle, and there was strength in numbers. Perhaps that was why the creature hadn't attacked the camp yet. And then I had an idea.

"What if I go?" I asked. "Sion and I aren't much help in a battle. We're still getting used to our bond. We can fly to the Conclave and deliver a message directly."

"That's a good idea," Henrik said.

I could see the hesitation in Anesko's eyes. Technically, I wasn't a member of the school and could leave or stay as I pleased, but once everything with Midia had been dealt with, I wanted to go back to the Citadel and be properly trained. In that spirit, I wanted to show Anesko that I could obey orders.

"Let me think about it," Anesko said. "It would be nice to get an answer, but I don't want to endanger you. If someone or something is stopping our messages, I don't want you getting caught up with it."

"Master?"

Everyone turned to look at Maren. She had slipped into the tent and stood near the opening.

"Yes, Maren?"

"My apologies for eavesdropping, but I couldn't help myself. I'll go with Eldwin to the Conclave. He and his dragon may not be formally trained, but Demris and I are. We can serve as Eldwin's guards in case there's trouble. And I've been to the Conclave before, so I know how to get there."

"That's a good idea," Henrik repeated.

"Yes, Henrik, I am aware that a lot of good ideas are being thrown around."

Anesko sighed and took a seat in an empty wooden chair beside the brazier. The room was quiet as he stared into the flames. I couldn't begin to fathom the amount of responsibility on his shoulders. As the silence continued to stretch, I felt Sion nudging my mind through the bond.

What's happening? She asked.

We might be leaving, I replied. *I'm waiting for Anesko's decision.*

Leaving? Her confusion flooded the bond, but I built a mental wall around the emotion and kept it from overwhelming me.

I'll explain later, I told her.

Anesko stood up and folded his arms across his chest. He scanned the room, looking at everyone present.

"I don't like it," he said. "The danger is unknown, but the same is true with being here. I'll allow you both to go to the Conclave. As soon as you arrive, send me a message. I want to know that you both arrive safely."

"Yes, Master," Maren said.

Anesko looked at me and I nodded. "Consider it done, Master."

"Get some rest for now. You can leave at first light. I'll have someone pack your saddles with provisions and make sure you have everything you need."

"Thank you," I said.

"You're both dismissed. The Curates and I still have more to discuss."

I followed Maren out of the tent. I had started to sweat and the cool night air was a welcome reprieve from the heat. We stood beside one another without saying anything. Maren grabbed ahold of my mangled hand and squeezed it briefly.

"I confirmed the rumors," she said. "My father is coming."

"That's good, isn't it?"

She shrugged. "It's good for the fight against Midia, though I don't know what men can do against whatever that thing is out there."

"We'll find a way to stop it at the Conclave, I'm sure of it," I said.

Maren laughed. "The Conclave is a bunch of crotchety old men who haven't done anything to improve the world with their power."

"If you don't think it'll help, then why are you going?"

She didn't answer immediately, but she turned to look at me.

"I lost enough time with you," she said. "I refuse to lose any more of it."

I smiled at her. "So, you're going for purely

selfish reasons, then?"

"Of course not," she replied. "I want answers as much as Anesko does. I've been listening to his meetings and found out that the other schools were supposed to send their riders here to join us. They aren't here. And now Anesko says the Conclave is non-responsive."

She was still the same woman. Breaking the rules, sneaking around … it was a total surprise to me that Master Pevus hadn't kicked her out of the school before he died. I was still convinced that her royal blood was part of the reason for that. She deserved to be a rider, had more than earned it, but I knew how the political circles of the nobles worked. Master Pevus himself had told Anesko that it would be foolish to think politics had no place in the Citadel. I pushed the thoughts away.

"How far is the Conclave from here?" I asked, changing the subject.

"If the wind is in our favor? Four hours without stopping. Can Sion fly that long?"

"We'll find out soon enough," I answered.

We parted ways and retired to our tents. I told Sion what tomorrow held and forced myself to get some sleep. It felt like I had just fallen asleep when I woke up to Maren tapping my shoulder.

"What is it?" I tried to hide my irritation at being woken up, but Maren didn't seem to notice.

"It's time to go," she said. "The dragons are saddled and everything is ready. Eat this." She handed me a wooden bowl filled with potatoes and eggs. "And be quick about it. I want to be gone before dawn."

I groaned. "The sun's not up yet?"

Maren's glare silenced any more of my complaints and I ate quickly. Her impatience was painfully obvious. Aside from the guards on watch, the camp was quiet. We mounted our dragons and left the camp behind, heading south. After two hours, we turned west and continued straight. We had to stop to allow Sion a break, which turned the four-hour journey into a six-hour nightmare.

By the time we reached our destination, I was ready to stretch my legs. My lower back was aching and I reached back to rub it. Sion sniffed the air and her scales tightened.

What's wrong? I asked. I scanned the ground below us, but I didn't see anything.

Magic, she replied. *Powerful magic was used here.*

I looked at Maren. Judging by her troubled look, Demris had sensed the same thing. Maren made a motion with her hand and both Sion and Demris began to descend. We landed in a clearing roughly a quarter-mile from an impressive tower made of white stone. I slipped out of the saddle and climbed off Sion's back. Maren walked over to me and I could see the concern etched onto her face.

"Sion told me magic was used here," I said.

"Dark magic," Maren replied. "I have no idea

what we're going to find when we get to the tower. There's a stable at the top for dragons, but once Demris alerted me, I figured it would be better to land out here instead."

"Good idea," I said.

"Those are the only kind I have," Maren said, smirking.

I rolled my eyes at her and we started our trek toward the tower, leaving the dragons behind. The landscape was flat and covered with tall golden-brown grass that swayed in the breeze. The tower sat atop a hill, high and imposing. As we topped the hill, the damage became obvious. The two massive oak doors that served as the entrance were wide open. Maren stopped and closed her eyes. She whispered arcane words under her breath, then snapped her head up.

"The wards are broken," she said.

"What do you mean?"

"There were powerful spells in place that protected the tower, but they're all gone."

"Someone undid the magic?" I asked.

"No. When someone unweaves a spell, there's only a faint trace of the magic that gets left behind. This was different. Violent, even. Imagine the wards as doors. They are opened and closed in a similar fashion."

"So, someone opened the door?" I asked, still not understanding.

"No … someone kicked it open."

2

"Is it safe to enter?"

I stared at the large oak doors. There was no telling what awaited us inside. I reached out through the bond and felt Sion's familiar presence. She couldn't fit inside the doorway, but it would have been more comforting if she were with me.

I am with you, Sion said. *If you encounter danger inside, I will know.*

Her words offered a small measure of relief.

"There's no way to know for sure," Maren replied. "You might want to be ready, just in case."

I drew my blade. Maren closed her eyes again and chanted softly. A faint iridescent barrier formed in the air in front of us. She opened her eyes and nodded in satisfaction.

"This will shield us from anything that comes at us head-on, but it won't last long."

"It's better than nothing," I said.

"Yes, it is. Ready?"

"As ready as I can be," I replied.

Maren led the way into the tower and I followed close behind her. The aroma of flowers drifted off her and I inhaled deeply, relishing the scent. We stepped through the doorway and I suddenly felt dizzy. I rested a hand on one of the doors while I waited for the feeling to pass.

"What was that?" I asked, scrunching my face as a wave of nausea faded.

"The Conclave technically doesn't exist in our world," Maren said. "The doorway is a portal. What you're feeling is the effects of traveling thousands of miles in a few seconds. The feeling shouldn't last too long."

"Good," I muttered before turning away from her and vomiting. I wiped my mouth with the back of my hand, feeling much better. "Does it not effect you?" I asked.

"A little," Maren answered. "I've been here before a few times, so I knew what to expect."

"You couldn't have warned me?"

She giggled. "What would be the fun in that?"

"Right."

I looked around the room. The place had been torn apart. Tables and chairs were overturned and books and parchments were scattered everywhere. It looked like a whirlwind had ripped through the place.

"They weren't expecting an attack," Maren said. "There's no signs of defensive magic anywhere."

"You said they were old men. Is it possible they just weren't paying attention?"

"No. I didn't care for any of them, but if there's one thing they're good at, it's attention to detail. They like to meddle in everything, so it doesn't make sense that they didn't see this coming."

"Let's hurry up and look around. This place gives me the creeps," I said.

Maren knelt and picked up some of the parchments and flipped through them. She shrugged and tossed them aside, then stood and walked to a spiral staircase that led up to the next level. The stairs weren't very wide, and we were forced to climb them single-file. They ended on the second floor and I spotted another staircase across the room.

"I've never been higher than this floor," Maren said. "This is where they conducted their meetings. Everything past this room will be new to me."

"It looks like no one is here," I said. "Do you think they fled after the attack?"

"It's possible, but I don't know where they would have fled to. There are only two other schools that I'm aware of, and if they went to one of them, we should have received word from them about the attack."

"Do you think they're dead, then?"

Maren looked at me but didn't answer. We searched the area, but it was in the same state as the room below and there was nothing of interest. As we neared the other stairway, however, I noticed a trail of blood.

"Look," I pointed. "Someone walked away from this."

Maren looked up the stairway, but because it too was spiraled, there was nothing to see. She seemed hesitant to go first, so I pushed past her and slowly made my way up. Drops of blood were on every stair. Whoever had been injured probably didn't make it very far. At the top of the stairs, the trail of blood ended. I looked around, but there was nothing.

"It's clear," I said.

No sooner had the words left my mouth and a clatter broke the silence. I gripped my sword hilt with two hands and cautiously moved toward the direction where the sound had come from. This room was darker than the others and I almost tripped over something. Maren laid a hand on my shoulder, stopping me. I looked back at her, but her eyes were closed and she had her right hand lifted high.

A hissing sound filled the air and a ball of light formed in her palm. It illuminated the room and revealed a grotesque scene. Bodies were strewn all over the place. I looked down and my eyes widened. The thing I had almost tripped over was a dismembered leg. I swallowed hard and continued forward, doing my best not to look at the gruesome sights. Another clatter made me startle.

"Who's there?" Maren demanded. "Show yourself!"

No one answered.

My heart was pounding in my chest. I stepped over the body of an old man, his lifeless eyes staring up at the ceiling, his mouth opened in a silent scream. Judging by the odd burns on his face and clothing, I assumed he'd been killed with magic. I nudged Maren and nodded down at him. There was fear in her eyes. We needed to get out of this place.

As we neared the next staircase, I saw a huddled form. I pointed my sword toward the person.

"Don't move," I warned.

There was no reply. Maren stretched out her hand and the glowing ball of light traveled away from her and toward the figure. The person was wearing dark blue robes and had their head hidden from my view.

"Councilor Flynn?" Maren said.

She hurried past me and knelt in front of the figure, then reached out and gently touched their hand. The person stirred and their hood fell back, revealing the haunted face of an elderly man. His hair was short and white with age. A thin, scraggly beard hung from his chin, the ends of it blackened and burnt.

"Who are you?" the man asked weakly.

"My name is Maren, an Adept from the Citadel."

"The Citadel? Has it fallen as well?"

"No," Maren answered. "Our riders are at the border of Midia waiting on the others."

"Midia? What are they doing there?" Councilor

Flynn coughed, his entire body shaking. When he stopped, there was blood on his lips.

"The king ordered an attack on Midia," Maren answered. "Master Anesko was sent approval from the Conclave."

"This is news to me," Flynn said. He struggled to sit up. I joined Maren's side and we helped him place his back against the wall.

"What happened here?" Maren asked. "Who did this?"

"Who indeed," Flynn replied. "That is a mystery. Whoever they were, they wielded spells I have never seen before. Our wards shattered like glass and before we could do anything, they were inside the tower, slaughtering everyone without mercy."

"We need to get him to a healer," Maren said.

"No," Flynn interjected. "Don't concern yourself with me. You must warn the others. Near the top of the tower, you'll find a well. Use it to send a message to the others. Tell them to prepare their defenses. The Conclave was their first target, but it won't be their last. Whoever they are, they seek the destruction of the riders."

"I'll send the messages," Maren said. "And then we're taking you with us."

Flynn pointed up weakly. His hand tremored and then fell into his lap. "Go," he said. "Time is too precious to wait."

"Stay with him," Maren told me. I nodded and she rushed up the stairs.

"What's your name?" Flynn asked.

"Eldwin," I replied "Eldwin Baines."

Flynn's face lit up in recognition. "Matthias's son?"

"The same."

"I see you followed in his steps."

"In a way, yes."

"When Master Pevus informed us that you'd left the Citadel, I wondered if our order would ever see you again. Your father was a brave man. If it wasn't for him, we might not have defeated the False King all those years ago."

"I'm not so sure he was defeated," I replied.

"Yes, I have also heard the whispers. I pray it is not true." Flynn erupted into another coughing fit, and this time there was more blood. A lot more. He began to wheeze as he breathed.

"Hurry, Maren!" I shouted.

Flynn grabbed ahold of my hand. His skin was cold.

"We grew lax in our strength," he said. "I fear we have made a mistake that we cannot fix. Do whatever you must to ensure that the riders stop what is happening."

I nodded.

"Promise me, son of Matthias."

"I promise," I whispered.

"My time grows short," Flynn said. "Death is waiting for me."

"No," I said. "We're going to get you to a healer. You're going to be fine."

Maren came down the stairs. "The magic has been destroyed," she said. "It's not working. Is there any other way to send a message out?"

I looked at Flynn. He was dead.

3

"This stinks of the False King," Maren said.

"Or the Necromancer," I replied.

"They are one and the same."

She was right. The Necromancer served the False King, so it was likely that the attack was their work. Flynn had mentioned that the attackers used spells he'd never seen before. I guessed that Flynn was in his late sixties, possibly early seventies. If he hadn't seen any magic like that in his lifetime, it made me scared to consider what we were dealing with.

Sion and Demris dug a hole in the ground near the tower and Maren and I laid Flynn to rest at the bottom. The dragons filled in the hole, and I stood at his makeshift grave, not knowing what to think.

"We need to get back to Anesko and tell him what's happened."

I considered Maren's words. Flynn had asked me to promise him that I would do whatever was necessary to stop the False King, and I was determined to keep my oath.

"If there's no other way to get a message out, then we need to deliver it ourselves."

"That's what I just said," Maren replied. "We need to leave now."

"I'm not going back to the camp," I said.

Maren grabbed my arm and turned me around. "What are you talking about?"

"Anesko has some idea of the trouble we're facing," I said. "The other schools are probably in the dark. What if Flynn is right? What if the attackers are going to target the schools next? I told Flynn I would do whatever was needed, so I'm going to warn the other schools. Perhaps I can convince them of the need to join Anesko at the border."

Maren stared into my eyes for a long while in silence.

"You know who you sound like?"

"No?" I said.

"Me."

"How so? I'm not breaking any rules by going."

"Maybe not, but Anesko wanted to know we arrived safely. If we leave to go to the other schools, he might assume we're dead."

"I thought about that," I said. "It doesn't matter what he believes if they don't get help, though. They'll all be killed by that creature."

"I'm not disagreeing with you."

"Good. Then we're going?" I asked.

"Of course. There's only one problem," Maren said.

"What's that?"

"We don't know where the other schools are."

"Yeah, I thought about that, too. Which is why I grabbed this." I held up a folded piece of parchment. Maren took it and opened it, then smiled at me.

"It's a map," she said.

"Yes, and it has the location of the other schools. I think the Terranese school is the closest to here. I figured we could go there first."

"Have you ever met a Terrenese person before?" Maren asked.

"I don't think so," I said. "I don't even know what that is."

"I met one of their diplomats in my father's court once. Their culture is radically different from ours, and so are their dragons."

"How different?" I asked.

"You'll see when we get there," Maren said with a smirk.

We ate a quick meal with the provisions Anesko had given us, then we mounted our dragons. Maren told Demris where to go and Sion and I followed his lead. We flew south, past farmlands and large cities, stopping every few hours to let the dragons rest. As we drew closer to the school, the landscape began to change into forested mountains. The air became warmer and the humidity was almost uncomfortable.

It took us a day and a half to reach the school.

Sion didn't complain vocally about her exhaustion, but I could sense her displeasure through the bond. I tried to send her soothing feeling but she ignored them.

When the school's fortifications became visible, I could understand what Maren meant when she said their culture was different. The architecture was vastly different from anything I'd seen. Stone posts and lintels supported large roofs that curved gently, giving the buildings a graceful appearance. They were beautiful structures.

I smell smoke, Sion said.

I scanned the area and realized why. The school was under siege. At first glance, I thought the shapes swirling around the school were birds, but as we got closer, the winged forms of griffons became obvious. A small army was encamped in front of the school, with rows of tents and siege weapons spread out strategically.

Before I could shout a warning to Maren, a host of griffons shot up from below us, clawing and snapping at our dragons' wings. Sion growled in anger and opened her mouth, filling the sky with flames. One unlucky griffon was hit directly, its feathers and flesh melting instantly. The smell was disgusting and I was thankful when the creature fell, taking its stench with it.

Demris roared and snatched two of the giant birds from the air with his claws. The crunch of their bones was so loud I cringed. Maren blasted another griffon from the air with a flash of magical lightning. The griffons were fast flyers, but they couldn't withstand the power of dragon breath. Flames and acid made short work of the remaining birds, giving us a clear path to the school.

Sion and Demris swooped down, picking up speed. I didn't see any more griffons coming, but it was hard to see as the wind stung my eyes. I put my head behind Sion's and braced myself for a rough landing. A cry rang out from the enemy camp and a volley of arrows came hurtling toward us. I gritted my teeth and waited to feel pain as they struck me. Before they got close, the air rippled around us and the arrows exploded, sending splinters and fletching in every direction.

We came at the ground fast, too fast, but at the last moment, it was as if some invisible force caught Sion and Demris and the dragons landed smoothly. More explosions sounded and I looked up to see another volley of arrows obliterated from the sky.

"Is that you?" I called out to Maren.

"No," she said, shaking her head.

"It's me," a female voice spoke.

The woman was short, possibly less than five feet in height. Her hair was long and black, held in place by a white ribbon. Her eyes were wide and slanted with dark brown irises. She wore an interesting set of armor that resembled dragon scales. She strode over to us with an air of authority.

"Identify yourselves, riders."

"I'm Eldwin Baines," I said as I climbed down

off Sion's back. "And this is Sion."

The woman looked at Maren.

"Maren Toft."

"Toft? So, it is true. The princess of Osnen is a rider?"

"I am," Maren confirmed. "Who are you?"

"My name is Curate Katori Sakurano. I don't intend to sound rude, but what are you doing here? Have you come with reinforcements?"

"We came to warn you of an attack, but it seems we are too late," Maren replied.

"So it would seem. What of the reinforcements? I sent my request for help to the Conclave days ago. What is the delay?"

"We have a lot to discuss," Maren said. "And we've come a long way. Is there somewhere else we can talk?"

Katori frowned but offered a nod. She shouted something I didn't understand and two men dressed in similar armor seemed to appear out of thin air. They approached Sion and Demris, but the dragons growled threateningly.

It's all right, I told Sion.

"Your dragons will be taken to the stables and cared for. Follow me," she instructed.

The Curate led the way into the exotic building. Maren trailed behind her and I took up the rear, giving Sion a reassuring glance as she was led away. The interior of the building was just as beautiful as the outside. Paintings of odd-looking dragons and people lined the walls, and the floors were made of wood. It was very different from what I was used to, but it provided a soothing environment.

"Where is your master?" Maren asked. "We'll need to speak with him as well."

"I'm afraid that won't be possible," Katori said.

"Why not?"

"Master Tsunejiro is dead."

"Gods," I groaned. "What happened?"

Katori gave me a look but didn't say anything until we reached what I thought was a dead end. She pushed on the wall and it slid open, revealing a room. I realized it wasn't a wall, but a door. The place was more surprising than I could imagine.

"Remove your boots and take a seat," Katori said.

I did as she asked and looked around, but there were no chairs. "Where do we sit?" I asked.

Katori smiled. "On the floor, of course."

"Right."

There were some of cushions on the floor surrounding a small tray with cups, so I picked one at random and sat down. I stretched my legs out and leaned back on my arms. Katori also sat on a cushion, but she folded her legs and sat up straight. Her posture felt so formal that I ended up sitting the same way. Maren sat beside me. She seemed to have some experience with the culture and suddenly became official in her demeanor.

"Master Tsunejiro was poisoned by a spy," Katori said.

"Our master was also poisoned," Maren replied. "One of our Curates is the acting master."

"Then we are in more of a similar situation than I thought. I am the acting master of this school. Please, tell me what is happening outside of these walls. I have heard nothing from the Conclave."

"The Conclave has fallen," Maren said. "We've just come from there. Someone attacked it and killed all the Councilors."

"This is bad news," Katori said.

"That's not all," I added. "The king has marched on Midia. Our riders went with the army, thinking the other schools were sending their riders. No one has arrived yet. I see why you haven't come, but we haven't heard from the other school."

"We did not receive any orders to go to Midia," Katori said. "Everything was normal until a few days ago when the army outside the walls suddenly showed up. It was as though they materialized from nowhere."

"Powerful magic is being used," Maren confirmed. "The spells at the Conclave were brutalized."

"What's the plan, then?" I asked. "How do we

sneak your riders past the army to get them to Midia?"

Katori laughed, a tittering sound that filled the room.

"Sir Eldwin, we are not going to Midia."

"Why not?" I asked. "Councilor Flynn's last words were to stop Midia at all costs."

"In case you haven't realized the gravity of our situation, there is an enemy at my door."

"I know. What is your plan to fight them or get past them?"

"We cannot do either," Katori said.

"If she's not going to send help, then we need to go to the other school," I said to Maren.

"I don't think you understand," Katori said. "You're stuck here."

4

"What do you mean we're stuck here?" I asked.

"There is no way out of the school except the front gates, and I don't intend to remove my wards. I haven't seen any magical attacks from the enemy, but that doesn't mean they don't have sorcerers in their midst. Judging by the supply wagons they have, I'm sure they have the supplies needed to wait us out."

"You're just going to stay here? Until when?"

Katori frowned. "It is the custom of my people to ensure we are not taken prisoner. If it comes to starving to death, then we will do what we must."

"I don't think that's necessary," Maren said. "What if there was another option?"

"I have considered every avenue," Katori said. "There is nothing we can do."

"We can help," Maren replied. "Eldwin and I have to reach the other school and get back to our master, and staying here until we die of hunger isn't going to work for me."

I looked from one woman to the other. It seemed that they both shared a similar trait. Stubbornness. I admired Katori's exotic beauty, but not in the same way I admired Maren. I looked around the room as they talked. There were no decorations or furniture at all. The walls were made of some sort of thin paper. It was a simple design, but functional.

I heard footsteps and saw the outline of someone approach the sliding door. Katori raised her hand, cutting Maren's words off.

"Enter," Katori said.

The door slid open and a young man bowed low. He had similar facial features as Katori, though they didn't appear related. He was wearing a form of armor that made him look like a formidable opponent.

A black cuirass made of steel covered his chest, and leather plates hung from the front which offered protection to his lower body and upper legs. Large rectangular leather plates adorned his shoulders, and his thigh guards were made of cloth and leather plates of varying sizes, each one connected to the other with small chains that had been sewn into the cloth. Under his arm, he held a helmet that had a dozen or more iron plates riveted together which included a lacquered metal face mask with the twisted visage of what appeared to be a demon.

I stared at the intricate details in awe. I tried to imagine what it would be like to see someone dressed like that coming toward me in battle. Given the mask, I'm sure it wouldn't be hard to believe a demon had stepped out of the underworld. Maren had been right. The Terranese culture was radically different than our own. Different, but intriguing.

"There is an emissary at the gates. He wishes to speak with you."

"Thank you, Domori. I will meet with him shortly."

Domori bowed again and slid the door shut, then left.

"What do you think they want?" Maren asked.

"Our surrender," Katori replied. "They will be disappointed. Would you like some tea?"

"Yes, please," Maren said.

Katori looked at me.

"Yes, thank you."

Katori nodded and grabbed the teapot off the tray and poured three wooden cups full. The teapot was adorned with dragons, but they were missing their wings. It raised my curiosity, but I managed to keep my questions to myself. I accepted a cup from Katori and took a sip. It tasted good and brought to mind a faint childhood memory that I couldn't quite remember.

"When are you going to speak with the emissary?" I asked.

"You are my guests. It would be rude to rush our meeting. The messenger can wait."

"May we go with you and listen to their demands? I'm curious to know what they'll say."

"You are welcome to listen, but you may not speak."

"Fair enough," Maren said.

Katori looked at me and I nodded in agreement.

"Very well. When you are ready, we will go and see what the snake says."

After Maren and I finished our tea, Katori stood up and put her boots back on and waited outside the room for Maren and me to do the same. She walked briskly down the hall and led us back out into the courtyard. Small fountains and trees with pink flowers decorated the area.

"Those are beautiful," I said, nudging Maren with my elbow and pointing.

"They are cherry blossom trees," Katori said. "My surname is derived from them."

We stopped in front of two large doors that towered at least fifteen feet in height. Katori slid open a panel on the door and peered through. I looked over her shoulder and saw a single man. He was holding a wooden pole that had a white flag attached at the top.

"I have a message from my lord and commander," the man said. He looked like the people I'd spent time with in Midia. If there had been any doubt left about who was behind the attack on the Conclave and who was directing this army, it was gone.

"Speak," Katori said.

"My lord has requested that you give him the two riders who just arrived, along with their dragons. He's also asked that you remove your wards of protection and open your gates and surrender peacefully."

I glowered at the man, but he kept his gaze on Katori.

"Is there anything else?" she asked.

"Yes," the man replied. "If you fail to comply with any of his requests, we will tear down your walls and burn everything and everyone to the ground."

"Tell your lord and commander that my answer is no, to all requests. Also tell him that if anyone comes near these walls, they will surely regret it."

The man hardened his stare. He didn't reply, but merely offered a curt nod and left.

"We must prepare our defenses," Katori announced. "My magic will only hold as long as my strength does."

"I have an idea," Maren said. "If you are willing to hear it?"

"We learn by listening," Katori replied.

"Do as the emissary requested. Lower your wards and open the gates."

Katori's face scrunched in confusion. "Where is the wisdom in that? You would have us all killed."

"It's a tactic my father has used in the past," Maren replied. "It's called the empty fortress. You open the gates and leave a few men on guard but send everyone else away. The enemy will think it's a trap and won't attack, at least not immediately. It will give us time to figure something else out."

"I will say that is clever, but what if they don't

think it's a trap and they attack? And where would I send everyone else? There is nowhere for them to go."

"There is a risk, of course, but the few times my father used the tactic, it didn't fail him."

"There is still a problem with sending everyone elsewhere. What is your idea for that?" Katori regarded Maren intently. I wasn't sure if Katori doubted it would work or not, but I had to agree with her that it was a clever idea.

"If they believe it's a trap and they hold off their attack, it will allow us to create a way out of here."

"I told you before, princess. This gate is the only way in or out."

"It is right now," Maren replied with a mischievous smirk.

Katori tilted her head, her curiosity apparent. "Explain."

"While the enemy is distracted by the apparent surrender, the dragons can burrow under the walls on the opposite side of the school. The work won't be seen, and once the tunnel is dug, it will also provide a way for the people to escape the city as well."

I could see the proverbial wheels turning behind Katori's eyes. She seemed about to approve but hesitated. "If we leave the school with no defenses, the enemy will destroy it."

"That's a possibility," Maren admitted. "But at

least this way, the riders and their dragons will escape with their lives. We can travel to the other school or we can part ways and you can lead your riders to Midia. Regardless of what comes after, staying here will be suicide."

"If we survive this, I will let your master know that you should be elevated to Curate. You've provided a way when I did not see one. I am indebted to you, princess."

"Please, call me Maren. I'm a rider first, royalty second."

"As it should be," Katori said. "Are either of you sorcerers?"

"I am," Maren replied.

"No," I said.

"Good, you can help me. I've got an idea of my own."

"'We learn by listening,'" Maren said, repeating Katori's own words.

"What about me?" I asked. "How can I help?"

"You will assist the other riders with moving supplies to the stables belowground. The catacombs below the school once had many openings into the forest outside the walls. It will be easiest for the dragons to tunnel through the ground there."

"I can do that," I said. "What are you two going to do, exactly?"

Katori looked at Maren and offered a grin of her own.

5

It wasn't long after the emissary returned to his camp with Katori's answer that the barrage of arrows began. Volley after volley flew high in the air, only to be blasted apart by the defensive magic that warded the school. It made me wonder why the enemy bothered until I remembered that Katori said the magic would hold as long as her strength did.

I worked with the man I'd seen earlier with the demon mask armor. Domori issued orders to everyone, directing what to take and where to put it. With surprising efficiency, the provisions and supplies needed for the escape were quickly gathered and placed within the catacombs below. I wanted to see the Terranese dragons, but Domori said it wasn't safe to go belowground while the dragons were tunneling.

Sion? I reached out through the bond.

I am here, she replied.

What do the other dragons look like?

There was a pause.

Sorry, I was trying to project an image to you, but it's not working. They are long and wingless. I don't know how they will fly when we leave.

Wingless dragons? I remembered the image on the teapot from earlier. Was it possible that dragons could fly without wings? It didn't seem likely, but a lot of things that never seemed possible had been proven otherwise recently.

Are you all right down there? I asked.

I feel like I'm suffocating, but I will be fine as long as I get to come aboveground soon. I'm not used to be being in the dark like this.

Satisfied that Sion was fine, I followed Domori into the school and up to one of the towers to watch the enemy camp. A large force of soldiers was marching toward the gates and ballistae were being loaded and moved into position. In the courtyard below, I couldn't see Maren or Katori, but I did see three riders standing by the gates.

"What are they doing down there?" I asked.

"Waiting for the signal," Domori replied.

"What signal?"

The air above the gates rippled like the surface of a pond. As soon as the ripples faded, the three riders pushed the gates open and took cover behind the wall.

"The wards are down," Domori said. "Now, we wait."

The sight of the open gates must have excited the enemy because they started to march faster. I started to doubt this plan was going to work. If the soldiers got through the gate, we'd be hard-pressed to get everyone out safely.

"Are the dragons still digging?" I asked.

Domori stared off blankly for a moment, then

said, "Yes, but they are close to breaking through to the surface."

I saw Maren and Katori enter the courtyard. Katori walked a few feet out of the gates and stopped. The approaching soldiers slowed their march. Maren lifted her hands in what I assumed was the beginning of spell. A few moments later, a thick fog began to form in the courtyard and slowly rolled out of the gates and into the surrounding area.

The fog quickly blanketed the landscape and obscured everything. Frightened cries rose from the enemy and I looked at Domori. His expression was serious, almost grim, but he kept his gaze on the scene below. As the fog continued to stretch out from the school, it began to thin enough that I could make out the forms of people running. There was no longer any order among the soldiers.

Other figures began to appear within the fog. Ghostly apparitions wielding weapons stalked the battlefield, terrorizing the enemy. When the soldiers tried to attack the apparitions, their weapons went right through the phantoms, causing the soldiers to turn and flee back to their camp. A horn blared and the remaining soldiers who hadn't fled in terror quickly retreated. Katori backed into the courtyard and the riders closed the gates.

"The tunnels are ready," Domori said. "We should go now."

He left, not waiting to see if I was following him. I watched Katori and Maren enter the school, then turned and made my way down to the entrance of the catacombs. The school grounds were practically deserted now. I waited for Maren and Katori to join me before going belowground.

"Those snakes will think twice before coming at the gates again," Katori laughed.

"That was an impressive display," I said.

"The fog was my doing," Maren said, "but the ghosts were all Katori."

Katori started for the catacombs. "We need to hurry. Our ruse bought us some time, but I doubt it will keep them distracted for too long."

I followed behind the two women into the dark tunnel. Maren summoned a ball of light to illuminate the darkness and we navigated our way to the others. Domori was waiting for us with a group of riders.

"Everything is prepared," Domori confirmed. "The dragons are ready to fly."

It took another ten minutes to reach the exit, which led up into the forest Katori had mentioned. The trees around us rose high into the air, the canopy overhead thick and bright green. The light that managed to penetrate the leaves gave off an odd hue of color. It was like something I'd seen in a dream once.

"The enemy still has griffons, but there aren't many," Katori said. "If they try to follow us, we'll need to deal with them."

"Are you coming with us to the other school?" I

asked.

"No," Katori answered. "I will lead my riders to Midia, since that was the will of the Councilor."

"We'll meet you there as soon as we can," Maren said. "Have you been to the other school before? Is there anything you can tell us that would help?"

"I have never been there, but I have heard that Hrodin can be a difficult man to deal with."

"Who's Hrodin?" I asked.

"He's the master of the school. The school is located high in the Wintersor Mountains. It is said that only the strongest can brave the journey to the school. Whether there is any truth to that, I do not know."

"Thank you," Maren said. "We will keep that in mind."

We stood in silence for a moment. I wasn't sure what else needed to be said, but Maren rushed forward and embraced Katori in a hug. The woman was surprised by the gesture. She awkwardly returned the hug and Maren released her.

"Safe travels to you and your riders," Maren said. "Can you give Master Anesko a message for us when you arrive?"

"Of course," Katori replied.

"Let him know we are safe and that we will return as soon as we can."

Katori bowed in reply and turned to Domori.

"Let's go."

I spotted Sion and Demris waiting in a thick patch of shrubbery, but I didn't see any other dragons. Maren climbed into Demris's saddle, but I looked around in confusion.

"Where's the Terranese dragons?" I asked.

As if in reply, the forest came alive with movement and I realized that the dragons had somehow camouflaged themselves in the foliage. I stared in amazement at the sight as the long lizard-like creatures took to the air. Sion had been right. These dragons did not have wings. Their bodies undulated from side to side like a fish swimming through water. I hurried onto Sion's back and she launched herself into the air.

We nearly slammed into one of the tall trees, but Sion managed to swoop to the right at the last moment. Demris and Maren shot ahead of us, taking the lead as we broke through the canopy. I looked back and watched as the sky filled with Terranese dragons. They were all lengths and colors. The smallest one I saw was at least twice the length of Sion. All of the dragons had lengthy whiskers that sprouted from their faces, much like wild cats I'd seen.

The way the dragons glided through the air reminded me of Katori. Foreign, but beautiful. A horn sounded from the enemy camp behind us and I turned to see griffons giving chase. A beautiful red and black dragon twisted around majestically and glided back to meet the giant birds. As it passed, I saw Domori riding on its back. He lifted his curved blade in salute. I held my hand up and silently prayed that he would make it to Midia.

Maren guided Demris north and we left Katori and her riders behind, heading for the Wintersor Mountains. I was worried about the master, Hrodin. If the rumors that said he was a difficult man were true, there was no telling how our meeting would go. We had managed to help Katori from a difficult situation and get them to aid with Midia, and it gave me hope that we would have the same luck with Hrodin.

Two days later, when we reached the base of the Wintersor Mountains, I was having different thoughts. The mountains stretched above the clouds and they were covered in snow. As we flew higher and the cold set in, I could see my breath when I exhaled. Sion complained about the temperature through the bond, and I had a feeling this wasn't going to be easy at all.

6

According to the map I'd taken from the Conclave, the school's name was Valgaard. It sat high upon a mountainside on a natural plateau that overlooked the rest of the mountains. By the time we reached the place and landed, Sion was heaving frantically. The air was thinner at this altitude, and it took every last ounce of strength for her to make it.

Demris was also affected, but he managed to hide his failing strength better than Sion. My clothes offered little protection against the biting wind and snow, and I could only imagine how Maren felt. I was slow to dismount from the saddle and my jaw shook so much that my teeth were chattering.

"We should have stopped to get warmer clothes," I said.

"We didn't have time," Maren replied. Her hands were shaking from the cold as she collected Demris's reins and I wrapped my arm around her shoulder, pulling her close as we walked together toward the castle. The dragons followed behind us, just as cold and miserable as I was. There was no defensive wall protecting the castle, but I doubted one was needed. It would be almost impossible to get an army up here, and I didn't think griffons were suited for this type of cold.

A lone guard stood near a small fire that burned without wood. I assumed the flames were powered by magic and marveled at the amount of energy it probably took to sustain it in this weather. I knew little about magic, but I had learned that it fed off your strength. As we got closer, I saw the man was tall, monstrously so. He was at least two feet taller than me, and he wore a thick fur pelt that draped his shoulders and reached down to his ankles.

The pelt had what appeared at first to be a hood before I realized it was actually a wolf's head. Judging by the size of the pelt, the wolf had to have been at least twice the size of a normal wolf. Resting against the wall of the castle next to him was a battle maul. The handle was metal wrapped with leather, and the hammer end was massive.

"Hail riders," the man greeted, raising a large hand. "What brings you to Valgaard?"

"W-we're h-here to see your m-master," Maren stuttered out.

"Do you have a message? I can deliver it for you."

"We have a message or s-sorts," I answered. "But it is for h-him alone."

The man regarded us with a skeptical eye. He grabbed ahold of his maul and lifted it, placing the hammer portion on his shoulder.

"Wait here," he said, then went inside the castle.

"He acts like it's n-not even c-cold," I muttered aloud.

Maren didn't reply other than to shrug. I looked back at Sion apologetically.

I need warmth, she said.

I know. I'll try to be quick in getting us inside.

Sion snorted, causing tendrils of breath to curl into the air from her nostrils. I heard the man crunching through the snow as he returned.

"Master Hrodin has agreed to see you. Come, I'll show you to the caves."

"The c-caves?" I asked.

"Where you can put your dragons," he said. "So they don't die out here."

I grew concerned about Sion's safety, but she snorted again.

Walk quicker, she complained.

I'm trying, but I can barely move my muscles, I replied.

Located around the castle, set in the mountainside, was the large entrance to a cave. The guard led us inside and a wave of warmth washed over me. The cave opened up into a huge chamber and the walls were lined with smaller openings. It reminded me of a honeycomb. A few dragons poked their heads out curiously.

"Those are empty," the man said, pointing with his hammer to a row of openings that were easily twenty feet above the cave's floor. Maren and I released the reins of our dragons at almost the same time, which I found funny. I struggled with my numb fingers to remove their saddles, then Sion and Demris walked past us and leaped into the air and entered the grottos.

"Will they be fed?" I asked.

"If you're here long enough," the man replied.

"I'm Eldwin," I said. "And this is Maren."

"I am Kell."

"It's pretty warm in here, but I don't see any fires," I said.

"It's magic," Maren replied. "Old magic."

Kell looked at Maren curiously. "You are a *völva*?"

"I'm not sure what that means," she replied.

Kell struggled to find another word and finally set his maul down. He placed the fingers of one hand into the palm of his other and made a sweeping motion. I knitted my brows in confusion, but Maren seemed to understand the gesture.

"A sorcerer," she said.

"Yes, a sorcerer," Kell said. "We call them *volur,* or *völva.*"

"I am a *völva,* yes."

Kell grunted, but I wasn't sure if it was good or bad. He lifted his maul, again placing the hammer end on his shoulder.

"Let the dragons rest. We go to see Master Hrodin now."

I was just starting to thaw and now we had to walk back out into the cold. As soon as we crossed the threshold of the cave entrance, the snow and freezing wind struck me full force. I let out a low cry and hunched forward, trying to shield my face. I kept my eyes on the ground and followed Kell's feet. We went back to the front of the castle and entered through a thick wooden door bounded with steel lining.

It was warmer inside the school, though not nearly as warm as the dragon stables. There was a chill in the air, but it slowly faded as we got further into the building. The stone walls and floor reminded me of the Citadel, but the similarity ended there. Where paintings would have been hung on the walls back home, animal heads and skins adorned them here. One of the heads was of a horned creature I had never seen before, with large black eyes and razor-sharp teeth that rivaled Sion's.

Kell took us down a long hallway that opened into a room with a throne. The chair sat upon a dais that lifted it a few feet above the floor, perhaps symbolic of the master's place above everyone else. Master Hrodin sat upon the throne, and two guards stood at each side. I had the impression we were visiting a king rather than the leader of another school. Kell bowed to the master and left.

Maren and I stood there silently, waiting for the master to speak. He stared down at us from his throne while he sheared the skin from an apple with a long dagger. The silence extended until it became awkward.

"Are we at the right place?" I whispered to Maren.

"Yes," she whispered back.

I didn't know what was happening, but I figured it was probably some sort of cultural thing as with the Terranese. We stood there so long my knees started to bother me. I lifted each leg up and down, stretching the muscles.

Are you in danger? Sion asked me.

No, I replied. *Just confused. How's the cave?*

Warm. Her contentment flooded the bond and I smiled.

Master Hrodin took a bite of the apple once he'd removed all of the skin. His crunching chews echoed throughout the room and my stomach growled in response. We'd stopped to eat before heading the rest of the way up the mountain, but our supplies were running low and we'd been forced to ration what we had left.

He ate almost the entire apple and tossed the core aside, then spun the dagger around and slammed the tip of the blade into the armrest of the throne and stood up. I had incorrectly thought that Kell was the largest man I'd ever seen. Hrodin was larger still. I guessed he was almost seven feet tall, and his muscles bulged under his armor. He wore a wolf's pelt similar to Kell's, but Hrodin's was as black as the night sky.

His breastplate was forged from steel and was decorated with the head of a dragon, its mouth open in a silent roar. I noticed a longsword sat propped up against the right side of the throne, easily within Hrodin's reach. The two guards wore steel breastplates with chainmail shirts underneath and held swordstaffs at the ready. They also wore backswords strapped at their sides.

Master Hrodin folded his arms across his chest and scowled.

"Give me a reason why I shouldn't kill you both where you stand."

7

This was a mistake.

Hrodin was the master of a school, so why would he threaten another school's students? The man had to be a fraud, perhaps a spy from Midia. Master Pevus and Master Tsunejiro had both been poisoned, so what were the odds that Master Hrodin hadn't met a similar fate?

"Excuse me?" Maren asked, breaking my train of thought. "Who do you think you're speaking to?"

I swallowed hard and looked at Maren, but she ignored me and kept her fiery glare on Hrodin.

"Look at how the little pup barks," Hrodin said, clapping one of his guards on the shoulder. "She's a spirited one, I'll give her that. Tell me something, riders. Why have you come to my domain without notice or permission? You're lucky Kell saw you struggling up the mountain, or Skarmundr would have ripped you apart."

I assumed Skarmundr was the name of a dragon. I was trying to draw Maren's attention, but she continued to ignore me. She took a few steps forward, still glaring at Hrodin.

"We are here to request your aid," she said.

Hrodin laughed heartily. "Is that so? Aid with what? And on whose authority did you come here?"

"I come with the authority of King Erling Toft,

and on behalf of the Conclave. Our enemy in Midia has risen and seeks our destruction."

Hrodin's laughter and merriment quickly faded and his face became a scowl again. "I don't answer to the king of Osnen, and I barely tolerate the Conclave."

He was being openly defiant against the king? I almost laughed myself. While Maren's father didn't directly control the dragon riders, it wouldn't be impossible for him to send his troops to leash Hrodin. It was clear that this conversation was above my head on many levels, so I kept my mouth shut and let Maren take the lead, which she was doing anyway.

"In that case, you may be relieved to hear that the Conclave has fallen."

Hrodin did well to hide his surprise, but for a brief second, I saw it in his eyes.

"You are lying," he said.

"On my honor as a rider, I speak the truth. Eldwin and I saw the destruction with our own eyes. Councilor Flynn was the only survivor, though he didn't live long."

Hrodin sat down on the steps of the dais and stroked his beard thoughtfully. He narrowed his eyes on Maren.

"How do you come with the authority of the king?"

Maren stood tall. "I am his daughter, Maren."

I didn't like the sudden interested look Hrodin gave her. I'd seen the same look on the faces of many other men. It was the same look that Jon had given her the day we first met. I clenched my fists at my sides, but I resisted the urge to say anything.

"What do you know of Valgaard?" Hrodin asked.

"Not much," Maren admitted.

Hrodin stood up. "Many ages ago, before the riders existed, Valgaard was home to my kin. The place was much different then. Where you see the tall mountains, there was once water as far as the eye could see. My kin had ships and they traveled the sea, ruling over everyone weaker than them. They grew a mighty kingdom."

I watched Hrodin warily as he walked toward us, but he stopped and pointed to the floor. The paint was faded, but there was still enough detail to see that there had once been a detailed map on the stones.

"When the dragons came, so too did magic. Powerful *volur* changed the landscape and the weather, sealing us away from the rest of the world. My people were forced to change their way of living, to adapt or die. As you can see, we adapted."

I listened intently. This was something I'd never heard before. Granted, I knew nothing about Valgaard anyway, but I had always assumed that dragons were here since the beginning of … everything. It seemed that might not be true.

"White dragons eventually came to make their home here because of the snow. They are hardy creatures and began to bond with my kin. We learned to ride them. And then the Conclave came and tried to force their rules upon us. We resisted at first and fought them, but their *volur* were too powerful to be defeated by our weapons of steel. Again, we were forced to adapt."

"That's an interesting tale, but I fail to see how it applies here," Maren said.

Hrodin smiled. "The reason Valgaard doesn't recognize the rule of Osnen's kings is that we were here first. My ancestors were kings, just as I am a king. My bloodline is purer than yours, princess."

I suddenly understood why Katori had said that Master Hrodin was rumored to be so difficult to deal with. If he thought himself a king, then he would act like one.

"This is no time to debate the legitimacy of who sits on the throne," Maren said. "The False King has returned. If we don't stop him now, then we are all doomed."

"No one has conquered Valgaard since its inception," Hrodin replied. "Every warrior here is worth ten Osnen men."

"That may be so, but you said yourself that *volur* could not be stopped by your weapons. A dark wizard is helping the False King, and he uses magic that hasn't been seen in a very long time. We need all the help we can get. If you won't hear my plea because of who my father is, then hear my plea as a fellow rider."

Hrodin was silent for a long moment. Judging by his attitude so far, I assumed he was going to decline the request and force us to leave.

"Who is your companion?" Hrodin finally asked.

"This is Eldwin Baines, son of Matthias Baines."

"I have heard the name," Hrodin said. "Are the legends about your father true?"

"As far as I know," I answered. "I was only a child when he died."

"Any man who dies in battle is a true warrior. As the son of such a man, you have my respect as a fellow warrior."

"Thank you, Master Hrodin," I said. "Will you help us?"

"I said you have my respect. I did not say that I owe you or the men or Osnen anything."

"Consider it a favor, then," Maren said. "A favor from one king to another."

Hrodin eyed Maren with that look that I despised, then turned around and walked back up to the throne and seated himself. He removed the dagger from the armrest and set the blade in his lap.

"I would have a word with you, princess." He looked at me. "Alone."

Maren turned to face me. I shook my head and

she frowned. "I'll be fine," she said.

"It wasn't a question," Hrodin said.

"Fine," I muttered.

I stalked out of the chamber and into the hallway we'd come through. Kell was there, leaning up against the wall, his giant maul resting on the floor.

"You have feelings for the girl," he said. It was a statement of fact and not a question.

"What does it matter?" I asked.

"It doesn't," Kell replied. "Not to me, anyway."

I stood next to him, quietly fuming on the inside. I decided I didn't just dislike Hrodin, I hated him. His pompous attitude reminded me of the nobles I'd dealt with my entire life. They thought they were better than everyone and treated lowborns like they were dirt to be walked upon. Well, I wouldn't stand for it. Not anymore. I was a dragon rider now.

As I was about to storm back into the chamber and give Hrodin a piece of my mind, I saw Maren coming out to meet me. She had a determined look on her face and I knew that whatever had happened, she'd made up her mind about something. I waited where I was and she looked at Kell.

"Master Hrodin wants to speak with you," Maren said to Kell. The big man picked up his maul and left.

"What did he say?" I asked.

"Let's take a walk," Maren replied. She grabbed ahold of my mangled hand and pulled me along as she walked.

"Is everything all right?" I asked.

"It will be," she said. "In time."

"What does that mean? Is Hrodin going to send his riders to Midia?"

"Yes, he has agreed to send his riders and his personal warriors to fight against the False King."

"That's good news," I said. "We did it, Maren. We rallied the schools and now we should have the strength to defeat that creature and the Necromancer."

"That's the hope," Maren said. She didn't sound as excited as I expected.

"What's wrong?"

We reached the end of the hall and she stopped walking. We were alone now. She turned to look at me and sighed.

"Please, tell me what's wrong."

Dread was starting to make my stomach curl and I could sense Sion probing my mind through the bond, trying to find the cause.

"Hrodin agreed to send his riders, but he has a stipulation."

"What does he want?" I asked.

Maren looked into my eyes and I could tell she was trying not to cry.

"He wants my hand in marriage."

55

8

"What?"

I couldn't have heard her correctly. Hrodin looked old enough to be her grandfather.

"It was the only way he would help," Maren replied. "Otherwise I would never have agreed to it."

All I could do was stand there in shock.

"This doesn't change anything," Maren said.

"This changes *everything*," I snapped.

"Marriages of convenience and opportunity happen all the time between royalty and nobles. That doesn't change how I feel about you."

Deep down, I knew she was just doing what she needed to for the people of Osnen, but that didn't make the feeling of betrayal sting any less.

"Yeah, well, if Hrodin thinks you have any care for me at all, I'm sure he'll keep you locked up here where I'll never see you."

"Eldwin," Maren said softly. "If you think anyone can keep me from doing what I want, then you don't know me at all."

I sighed and lowered my gaze to the floor. "I'm sorry," I said.

"Don't be. I can understand why you're upset. I

would be too if our roles were reversed."

Maren placed a hand under my chin and forced me to look at her. "Nothing is ever set in stone. It's only an agreement right now. I told Hrodin that I will not speak of the matter until the False King is defeated. It gives him an incentive to get what he wants."

I looked down the hall towards the throne room, my anger still burning.

"Let's forget about it for now," Maren said. "We've been given rooms to stay in and we can leave first thing tomorrow morning."

Forgetting that the woman I was falling in love with was now engaged to another man would be a task far easier said than done. Yet, she was right. What could be done about it right now? I didn't want to spend the night in Valgaard, but after two days of travel, it was better than sleeping in the snow.

Kell came down the hall and paused a few feet away.

"We've got company," I said.

Maren turned around and motioned to him. He closed the distance and set his maul on the floor.

"I've been instructed to show you to your rooms," Kell said.

"Do you have hot water for a bath?" Maren asked. "We've been on the road for a while and I smell like a dead horse."

Kell chuckled, a peal of deep-chested laughter. "We do," he said. "Come, I'll show you the way."

The big man led us up to the second floor of the castle. Maren's room was beside mine, and down the hall was a shared bathing room. It was quiet and there didn't appear to be anyone else staying in the same hall.

"I'll have someone fill the tubs for you," Kell offered. "The buckets of water are heavy and by the time you got the tubs full, the water would be cold."

"Thank you," Maren replied.

Kell nodded and left.

"I'll let you go first," I said. "Just let me know when you're done."

I went into the room I'd been given and slipped my boots off, then quickly put them back on when my feet touched the cold stone floor. I walked over to the bed and touched the pillows. They were filled with feathers and soft to the touch.

The bed itself was massive, easily big enough to hold five people comfortably. The posts at each corner of the bed were thick and came close to touching the ceiling. Upon closer inspection, I found they were actual tree trunks. There was an empty chest at the foot of the bed made of the same wood, but no other decorations or furniture. A hearth was set in the wall opposite the bed and I built a small fire, then sat in front of it.

As I soaked up the warmth, I could feel my eyes getting heavy. I was dozing off when I heard a knock at the door. I got up and opened the door to find Maren standing there, her hair still wet.

"I'm freezing now," she complained.

"I'm sorry. I built a fire if you want to warm yourself. I'm going to clean up before the water gets cold."

I left Maren in my room and hurried to the bathing chamber. Thankfully, the water was still warm. I unclothed and washed the grim off my skin, then laid back and relaxed. The warm water helped to ease the soreness in my muscles. I closed my eyes and sought out Sion's mind through the bond. She was asleep, so I didn't bother her. I stayed in the tub until the water started to get cold, then got out and dried myself off and put my clothes back on.

When I stepped back into my room, Maren was still there. She was sitting in front of the fire and I could tell by her drooping eyes that she was about to pass out. I knelt beside her and pushed a strand of hair behind her ear.

"Go get in your bed," I whispered. "Before you fall asleep on the cold floor."

Maren gave me a lazy smile. I stood up and offered her my hand, then pulled her up to her feet. She walked over to my bed and climbed into it, using the large animal pelt on the bed to cover herself.

"I guess I'll take your room," I said.

"No. Get up here and keep me warm."

I hesitated for a moment but did as she asked. I laid beside her and she snuggled closer. She yawned, which made me yawn. It was late afternoon, but I was exhausted. I figured we could take a short nap and then eat dinner.

"Hrodin said he'll need a full day to mobilize his riders," Maren whispered sleepily. "That gives us a full day together without him."

"Good," I said.

That was the last thing I remembered before I woke up from a nightmare. Sion's memories of her tortured imprisonment under Rory's wizard had flooded the bond again. I managed to seal my mind from the dark images, but I was wide awake. The fire had died down and only embers glowed in the hearth, but I was too comfortable to get up and add wood.

I glanced around the room, but there were no windows, so I had no idea how late it was. I laid there for a long time, staring up at the ceiling while my mind ran a hundred miles a minute. I thought about Esmond and Altin. One was a tortured soul, trapped by the Necromancer's power and the other was a willing follower of the False King. Even though they were my enemies, I hoped they were all right.

Eventually, I fell into a fitful sleep, tossing and turning more than anything. I opened my eyes and saw Maren was gone. I sat up and looked around, but she wasn't in the room. I laid back down and stretched, forcing the fogginess of sleep from my brain. I could feel that Sion was awake and she was humming with satisfaction.

Food, she said.

Is it still dark? I asked her.

No. Dawn draws near.

Good. We'll be leaving soon. We're going back to the border.

The other dragons said they are flying to battle.

We all are, I replied. *It's time to stop the False King once and for all.*

What of the creature?

I wasn't sure what to say. *I ... don't know. I think with enough riders, we'll be able to defeat it.*

Let it be so, Sion said.

The door opened and Maren stepped inside.

"You're awake," she said. "I brought you something to eat. It's almost time to leave."

She brought a wooden plate to the bed and set it down. There was half a loaf of bread and an apple.

"I already ate, so this is all for you," Maren said.

"Thanks." I sat back up and pulled a piece of bread free and tossed it into my mouth. It was warm and fresh. After I finished eating, I rolled out of the bed and put my boots on and strapped my sword around my waist.

The castle was full of movement as we headed for the stables. It seemed all of the people in

Valgaard were similar in stature to Kell. They also wore the same style of armor, but each person had their own style of decoration.

Sion and Demris were waiting eagerly for us. Someone had saddled them already. I climbed up Sion's shoulder and got settled, then waited for Maren and Demris to lead the way. The snow had stopped falling, but the temperature was still ungodly cold.

"Back to Midia," Maren said.

Demris exited the cave and leaped into the air. He struggled against the wind for a moment, then leveled out. Sion followed him and the wind whipped my clothes around violently. The quicker we got away from this hellish landscape, the better. We flew past the castle and down the mountainside. I watched the landscape steadily change as we got lower. Once we reached the base of the mountains, we turned northeast and flew straight.

After a few hours, I noticed Sion was sniffing the air curiously.

What is it? I asked.

I smell griffons, she replied.

I scanned the sky, looking in all directions. And then I spotted them. They were behind us, quickly closing the distance.

I'll turn around and burn their wings off, Sion said.

No, keep going. Fly faster, if you can.

I do not fear those tiny birds.

I don't doubt that, I said. *It's not a matter of fear. It's a matter of survival. We're outnumbered.*

How many? Sion asked.

At least thirty.

The griffons were on us before we were fully prepared.

Sion flew ahead of Demris and I waved my arms frantically at Maren to get her attention, then pointed behind her. She looked over her shoulder, then back at me and her face grew dark. Several of the birds zipped past me, snapping their talons at Sion's wings. Their armored riders wielded lances, and one almost struck me in the arm. The near strike sent a chill of fear down my spine.

Fly faster! I urged Sion.

I'm trying! She roared and swiped at a passing griffon with her claw. She didn't hit the bird directly, but she smacked its flank hard enough that the bird lost control and spiraled downward a few feet.

We were surrounded by griffons on all sides. The birds nipped and clawed at Sion and Demris, enraging the dragons further. I drew my sword and swung awkwardly from the saddle at the rider of a passing bird. The sword clanged against the person's back and I nearly lost my grip on the hilt of my blade.

Get low! Sion warned.

I put my sword across my lap and leaned as far forward in the saddle as I could. A wave of heat filled the air as Sion breathed flames, setting several griffons on fire. Their squawking cries of pain hurt my ears. I sat back up and swung at another rider. Sion jerked unexpectedly and my blade missed the rider but cut a deep gash into the griffon's hind leg.

"Fly closer!" Maren shouted.

She had a ball of flame the size of a small rock in her hand. I told Sion to do as Maren said and she drifted to the left, getting as close to Demris as she could without disrupting his flight. A pale blue light filled the air around the dragons, shielding us within a protective sphere. Maren stood up in the saddle and hurled the ball of fire into the air. The shield opened to let it pass through and sealed closed.

I watched the ball continue upward for a short distance, then gravity took over and it began to fall. As it descended, it grew exponentially and then exploded. A wave of flame filled the sky around us, held at bay by the glowing shield. My eyes widened in shock. It was like being in the center of a wind dervish, only the wind was replaced by raging flames. Griffon and rider alike screamed in agony.

The flames faded and the sky was clear of enemies. I glanced down and saw their bodies falling. The shield around us flickered briefly and then dissipated.

"That was incredible!" I shouted, looking at Maren. She'd gone unconscious. Her body slumped to the side and she slipped free of the saddle, free-falling through the air.

9

Sion dove down sharply, forcing me to grip the saddle horn with my left hand to keep from joining Maren in the air. My stomach clenched and I thought for sure I was going to lose my breakfast. Sion brought her wings in tight to her body and she passed under Maren, catching her somewhat roughly on her scaly back.

I quickly sheathed my blade and scrambled out of the saddle, then grabbed onto Maren's hands and pulled her into my lap. Her chest rose and fell with her breathing, but she was otherwise unresponsive.

We need to find a healer, I told Sion.

Demris says there's a city close. He'll lead us to it.

Maren's dragon shot ahead, flying faster than anything I'd seen before. I held onto Maren tightly as Sion picked up speed to keep up with Demris. The fact that Maren was breathing was a good sign. I could only guess as to why she was unconscious, but I assumed that she must have overexerted herself with the fire spell.

She'd taken out close to thirty griffons and their riders, which was no small feat. I hugged her close and pressed my lips to her ear.

"You're going to be fine," I whispered over and over. I desperately hoped my words were true. I was so consumed with worry that I barely noticed when

Sion began to descend.

How is she? Sion asked.

I'm not sure. She seems all right, but ...

Demris says we should land outside the city. What do you want me to do?

Get as close as you can, I told her.

She soared in wide circles around the city, slowly descending and finally landing outside the city's border. I hefted Maren over my shoulder and jogged toward the gates. A couple of bored-looking guards glanced my way but didn't try to stop me. The streets were busy with people shopping and selling. I was having trouble seeing the signs on the buildings and Maren was starting to get heavy.

I rushed into the first inn I came across and booked a room, then took Maren upstairs and laid her in the bed.

"I'll be back," I promised her.

Can Demris still feel Maren through the bond? I asked Sion.

There was a pause, then Sion replied, *Yes.*

Tell him I'm leaving her in a safe place, but if he senses anything wrong, he should let you know.

He said if he senses anything wrong, he'll burn the city to the ground.

That was fair enough, but I doubted anything would happen to her. I left the inn and navigated my way through the crowded streets, trying to find a healing shop. There were tons of inns and I even passed a brothel, but I wasn't having any luck finding what I needed.

Is there a rider presence in this city? I asked Sion.

Demris said no.

Great. If I couldn't find a healer, then I needed to find a wizard. Maybe a magic user would be better suited to figure out what was going on with Maren anyway. I asked a passerby for the location to the sorcerer's guild and the man spouted off the directions so quickly I didn't quite memorize them all, but with a little exploration, I ended up finding the place.

The interior was dark, and I had to wait for my eyes to adjust to the gloom. A man in thick brown robes looked up from the book he was reading when I stepped inside.

"Greetings," he said.

"I need help. My friend is unconscious."

"That's not good. What happened?"

"I think she expended too much energy casting a spell," I said.

"That's probably what happened. Is your friend a member of the guild?" he asked.

"I'm not sure. Maybe?"

"What's her name?" The man opened a different book and looked at me.

"Maren. Maren … Toft."

"The princess of Osnen?" The man seemed impressed. "You're in good company, considering."

"Considering what?" I asked.

"Your deficiency."

"My what?"

"Your arm."

I sighed and tried to be patient. "Can you help her or not?"

"Let me see if she's in our records," the man replied. He flipped toward the end of the book and began scanning the pages. After a long moment, he cleared his throat. "She's not listed in here."

"What does that mean?" I asked.

"It means we can't help. If she comes to, you should suggest to her that she join the guild."

"*If?* What do you mean *if* she comes to?"

The man closed the book and set it aside. "When someone goes too far with magic, it can cause problems. Those problems can be temporary, or they can be permanent. In rare cases, it can mean death. It depends on what someone does and how much extra energy they use."

I shook my head. "You can't help someone because they aren't part of your club? What kind of nonsense is that?"

"Why doesn't someone from the royal court take a look at her?"

I stared at the man as if he were insane. We weren't anywhere near the capital, so how exactly did he expect someone from the court to help? I rolled my eyes and left the building. I could fly back to the camp at the border, but if Maren needed help, that could likely be a bad idea. There wasn't much I could do at this point, so I decided to head back to the inn and check on Maren.

Along the way, I became aware of someone following me. They did well to hide their pursuit at first, but when I turned down an empty street and two people followed at a distance, I knew what they were doing. I picked up my pace, hoping to throw them off my trail, but I took another side street and ran into someone.

"Sorry," I said, keeping my gaze on the ground. I tried to go around them.

"Well, well, well," a familiar voice said, grabbing me by my mangled hand. "If it isn't the thief."

I looked up into Rory's face and thought for sure my heart had skipped a beat.

"Rory," I finally managed to say. "What are you doing here?"

The two people that had been following me joined us. A glance over my shoulder revealed it was Vance and Geoff. Of all the possible people to run into …

"It looks like our luck just changed," Rory said to Vance. "The man who bought the dragon you stole is here and he wants to know where his prize is."

"Let go of me," I snapped. I tried to pull my hand away, but his grip was like an iron shackle. Geoff and Vance stepped in close and grabbed me by my arms.

"Listen here," Rory said. He cleared his throat and turned his head to spit. "You're going to pay a visit to our employer and tell him why we don't have his dragon. And then you're going to pay him back so he doesn't kill us."

"And what makes you think I'm going to do that?" I asked. "What if I just call my dragon and have her tear you to pieces?"

Rory smiled at me as he unsheathed a dagger and pressed it against my neck. "Well, for starters, I don't think your dragon can get here before I slice your throat. And secondly, if I didn't gut you, I doubt you'd want innocent blood on your hands. If you called your dragon into the city and she burned down the entire block … well, you'd be responsible for all of it."

I cursed him in my mind. He was right. If there was one thing I learned about Rory while traveling with him, it was that he was clever. The look of defeat must have been obvious on my face because Rory laughed in triumph.

"Let's get this mess over with," he said.

Vance and Geoff led me through the city to a one-story plain building. There were a couple of people I assumed were mercenaries standing near the entrance, as well as Rory's wizard. I tried to remember his name, but it eluded me.

"How did you know I was here?" I asked.

"We didn't," Rory said. "Not exactly. We've been tracking you since you left, but it was difficult for a while. You must have been far from here."

I wasn't going to divulge any information to him willingly, so I kept my mouth shut about where I'd been. "You tracked me? How? I haven't traveled by foot in a while."

"Wizards don't track footprints, fool," Rory grunted. "They use magic."

As if on cue, Rory's wizard walked over to us. "You see? I told you it would work."

"What would work?" I asked.

"The tracking spell. You see, all I needed was something you touched that I could hold in my hand."

The wizard motioned to one of the mercenaries and they disappeared into the building, then returned carrying something draped under a piece of cloth.

"It was too easy," the wizard chuckled. He removed the cloth. I had completely forgotten about the item he held.

It was the music box.

10

Vance and Geoff escorted me along the cobblestone street and stopped a short distance away from a structure that had several armed men guarding the entrance. Vance pushed me forward and then hung back with Geoff.

I didn't know how I would get out of this predicament, but I needed to hurry and get back to Maren. I slowly walked up to the entrance and the guards stepped in front of me, blocking the way. One of them broke away from the others and stepped forward. He was about the same height as me and had an old-fashioned handlebar mustache.

"This area is off-limits to the general population," he said gruffly.

All of the men had their hands resting on the hilts of their swords, including the apparent leader of the group.

"I'm here to speak with your leader about the … uh, dragon," I said.

The man tilted his head to the side, suddenly interested. "The dragon, you say? Good, good. The delivery is late. Are you a messenger of Rory's?" he asked.

"Of a sort," I replied.

"Right. Well, follow me, then."

The man turned around and the other guards

moved to the side to let us through. I followed the leader, glancing around curiously at their mini fortress. Aside from missing the towers and grand décor, the gray stone building looked like it had started to be a castle but was never completed.

Inside, I saw at least fifty other men. They were all armed like the men outside, and I was beginning to wonder what sort of man Rory had gotten himself involved with. None of the men looked at me as we passed them, which told me they either weren't very curious or they didn't even notice me.

We entered a large room that had a long table with a map stretched out on its surface. Tiny wooden figurines were scattered all over the map. Standing at the head of the table was a woman. She wore a chainmail shirt over a black tunic and had matching colored pants. A sword was strapped at her hip. She looked up as we approached.

"Rory sent a messenger about the dragon," the man said, nodding toward me.

"Excellent. Have you seen Cedric?"

"No, my lady."

"If you do, send him my way."

The man bowed and left. I stared at the woman uncertainly. She had dark black hair and green eyes, and a faint scar ran the length of her left cheek. She was a lowborn like me, but she exuded an authority that led me to believe she wasn't a random mercenary.

"Who are you?" she asked.

"I'm Eldwin," I replied. "Eldwin Baines."

The woman rose a slender brow. "Are you related to Matthias Baines?"

I nodded.

"He was a good man. Better than most."

"That's what I've heard," I said.

"I'm Seren Gray, leader of this band of misfits."

"It's nice to meet you," I replied.

"So, where's Rory? Did he lose my dragon? I'll have his head on a pike if he did."

"It's a bit of a long story, but I can explain," I said. She was clearly the rough type, possibly violent, and if there was any weight behind her threat of beheading Rory, I didn't want to be on the wrong end of her anger.

"Start explaining," Seren said.

"I was a guard with Rory's caravan and I sort of ended up bonding with the dragon."

"Sort of?"

"I bonded with the dragon," I clarified.

Surprisingly, Seren's face remained impassive. "I see. And where is the dragon now?"

"She's outside the city. My friend and I were on our way to the border when we were attacked by griffons."

"I've received reports from my men that there were griffons in the area, but to be honest, I didn't believe them. Any idea what they're doing in Osnen?"

"They attacked the schools," I said.

"You're joking," Seren replied. "Midia thinks their birds can stand a chance against dragons?"

"I wish I were joking. The Conclave has fallen and the Terranese had to abandon their school. They flew to the border to join the Osnen riders. Hrodin from Valgaard is the only one who has gone unscathed."

"Naturally," Seren replied. "Their fortress is on the top of a frozen mountain. It wouldn't make sense for the Midian's to go there."

Seren seemed to know a lot about the schools. I wanted to ask her why, but I wasn't sure how to bring it up. She must have noticed my uneasiness.

"Speak your mind," she said. "I'm not easily offended."

"How do you know about the details of the rider schools?"

"I used to be one," Seren replied. "I rode a silver dragon before she fell in battle against the False King ten years ago." Seren's facial expression turned wistful for a brief moment, but her stoicism quickly returned.

"I'm sorry to hear that," I said. "Why did you buy a dragon if you already bonded with one previously?"

"You've been told that you can only bond with

one dragon, yes?"

I nodded.

"What if that weren't true? What if that was an exaggeration or even a lie?"

I shrugged. "So what if it's not true?"

"If it wasn't true, then those of us who've lost a dragon could bond with another. It wouldn't replace the original bond, but I'm sure I wouldn't feel so empty."

"You bought the dragon to see if that was true or not," I said, following her logic. "And what if it was true?"

"Then I would have let one of my men bond with it. A dragon is a powerful ally, even more so when it is outside the control of the Conclave."

"Is that even allowed?" I asked. "A rider not bound to the school?"

Seren scowled. "Does it matter? The Conclave can't keep their control over the dragons forever. Especially now."

She had a point, but still. There were reasons that rules were in place. Seren reminded me of Maren. Neither of them cared for the rules.

"What of your friend?" Seren asked. "Is he a rider also?"

"She," I corrected. "And yes, she is. She was injured in our fight, but it's not a normal injury. I think she pushed herself too far and now she's unconscious."

Seren looked at me curiously. "What do you mean?"

"She's a sorcerer."

"I see."

"I'm only here because I was trying to find a healer for her. I ran into Rory and he forced me to come here to repay you since the dragon bonded with me."

Seren snorted. "Rory's an idiot. Unfortunately, I learned that a little too late into the game. Don't worry about repaying me. I knew your father, and he would be proud to know you've followed in his path. I employ several sorcerers and a healer. I'll have them check on your friend."

"Thank you," I said. I offered an awkward bow, not sure how to express my thankfulness.

"I've heard rumors," she said, changing the subject. "Maybe you can tell me if they are true. People are saying the False King is back. Do you know anything about that?"

"It's true," I replied. "And apparently, he has a powerful sorcerer working with him. The riders are gathering at the border to launch an attack on his castle."

"I thought we stopped him before," Seren said.

"Everyone did. Either he did well to fake his death, or this sorcerer is behind his resurrection. His followers call him the Necromancer."

"Interesting."

"You said you fought against him before. Will you join the battle again?"

"No," Seren said without hesitation. "I did my part. It's time for others to fill the gap. People like yourself."

I didn't know what to say to that.

Again, Seren changed the subject. "Where's your friend? I'll send a sorcerer and my healer now."

"She's at an inn near the city's front gates. I don't know the name of it, but the sign had a rose with wings."

"I know the place," Seren said. She motioned to a guard standing in the shadows that I didn't even notice was there. "Go get Taren and Helena. Tell them to go to the Rose and Wing immediately."

"Thank you again," I said after the guard left. "How can I repay you?"

"You can't," Seren said. "And I'm not asking for restitution, anyway. Consider it a favor from one rider to another."

I remembered the fear Rory and Vance had concerning their employer, but they had mentioned that *he* would kill them. If Seren was a woman, why did they refer to her as a man?

"Have you met Rory?" I asked.

"Not directly, no. Why do you ask?"

"He thinks you're a man," I said.

"Understandable. Not many women have the fortuity I've experienced. Go see to your friend. And take care of your dragon. You can't imagine the heartache of losing one."

"I will," I said. "What about Rory? He won't let me leave, not if he thinks everything hasn't been cleared up in his favor."

Seren smiled. "I'll take care of Rory."

11

I arrived back at the inn to find two robed people waiting in the common room. They were talking amongst themselves and went quiet when I walked up to them.

"Taren and Helena?" I asked.

"Yes," one answered. They were both women, so I wasn't sure which was who.

"Taren?" I asked of the one who spoke.

"Very good guess," Taren replied with a smile. "Your friend is ill?"

"Not quite," I said. "She cast a spell and passed out, but she hasn't awakened yet."

"Take us to her," Taren said. The tone of her voice turned urgent.

I led them upstairs and unlocked the door. Taren hurried past me, Helena right behind her. I stepped into the room and saw Taren was holding Maren's arm up, two fingers on her wrist.

"Her pulse is strong," Taren confirmed.

"That's a good sign," Helena said, looking over her shoulder at me.

That was a relief. I wasn't sure what to expect when it came to magic. The two women spent the next few minutes doing all sorts of odd things like plucking a hair from Maren's head and waving their arms over her body.

"Your friend will recover just fine," Taren said. "She'll need some rest, even after she wakes up, but other than being weak, she didn't suffer any lasting effects from the magic."

"Thank the gods," I breathed. "And thank you, ladies, for coming."

"Just following orders," Taren replied. "I'm not sure how you know Seren, but she doesn't send her personal healer to just anyone. You must be highly regarded by her."

That was an interesting bit of information. I shrugged, not knowing what to say. The two women left the room and I followed them downstairs. After they left, I ordered some food and asked the barkeep to bring it up to the room, then returned to Maren's side. The food arrived just as Maren's eyes fluttered open. She looked at me with a confused expression. I opened the door and accepted the tray of food, then shut the door and brought the tray to the bed.

"Where are we?" Maren asked. Her voice was soft and feeble.

"We're safe," I said. "You passed out after fighting the griffons and Demris led us here to get help. I thought you …" I couldn't say it. I put some food onto a plate and handed it to her. "You should eat something. Taren said you'll make a full recovery."

"Who's Taren?" she asked.

"It's a long story," I replied. "I'll explain later."

Maren ate slowly and I helped her with drinking some water. After getting some food into her system, the paleness in Maren's face began to fade.

"We need to get to Midia," she said.

"We will, but not today. You need to get some rest. One more day isn't going to make a difference."

"Not that you know of," Maren replied. "The battle could be raging right now for all we know."

"Possibly," I agreed. "But in your weakened state, you won't do anyone any good."

Maren sighed in defeat and rolled onto her left side so that she was looking at me. "What happened? My thoughts are a little foggy."

"You killed everyone with a fire spell."

Her eyebrows rose in surprise. "Seriously?"

"Yes," I said. "It was quite a display, but then you went down. Literally. You fell out of your saddle and Sion had to dive down to catch you."

"It sounds like I missed the best part of the action," Maren said, smiling.

I rolled my eyes at her. "If you say so. Get some sleep. I'm going to take a walk around the city."

Maren nodded and rolled to her other side. I left the room and locked the door behind me, then exited the inn and walked along the street. There were still many people clogging the pathways, but I found a side street that was practically abandoned. All of the buildings were in serious need of repair and none of them seemed to be in use.

As I walked past one of the structures, a man stepped out of the doorway and grabbed my arm. It startled me and I jerked away, which almost caused me to fall. I caught my balance and glared at the man. He looked crazy. What was left of his hair was matted to the side of his head and his eyes were wide.

"Have you found her?" he asked. His accent was thick and I almost didn't understand him.

"I'm sorry, I don't know what you're talking about."

"My wife. She died and I can't find her."

I took a step back. The man was clearly not in his right mind and I didn't want any trouble from him.

"I went to the island to look for her, but she wasn't there."

"What island?" I asked. I figured if I indulged him for a bit, he would leave me alone. I also assumed that he was referring to his wife's body. Perhaps whoever had his wife had taken her to an island somewhere.

"The Island of Lost Souls," he replied. "Have you been there?"

I shook my head. "No, I'm sorry. I've never heard of it."

"Never heard of it? It's the only place to find those you've lost. It took me a long time to get to the island, but my wife wasn't there. She must have passed beyond the veil."

I still wasn't sure what the man was talking about, but I kept a smile on my face and nodded.

"The veil of what?" I asked.

"Of the in-between," the man replied as if I should know. "When someone dies, sometimes their soul is trapped between this mortal existence and what lies beyond. They go to the Island of Lost Souls until someone finds them."

"Where is this island? And how do you reach it?" My curiosity was slightly raised, but I honestly thought the man was babbling. Grief can ruin a person, and while I understood what it was like to lose someone, I didn't believe that living in perpetual mourning was how to get past the loss.

"There's only one way to get there," he said. "The ferry. The helmsman requires payment, but if you have what he seeks, he'll take you to the island."

"And what does he seek?" I asked.

"You'll know when you get there. When he asks for it, you'll know whether you have it or not."

"Right. Well, I should get back to my friend. She's not feeling well, so I should probably check on her. Take care of yourself, sir. I'm sure your wife would want you to."

"She would, yes," the man said thoughtfully. "If you ever go to the island, be careful. Things there are never what they seem."

"Thank you for telling me."

The man went back into the dilapidated building and I hurried back onto the main street. No wonder it had been deserted. There was an irrational man accosting people at random. I walked along the busy street, seeing what there was to see down the merchant's area before turning down another side street. Unknowingly, I found myself back on Seren's street. The building where Rory had taken up shelter was curiously vacant.

I stepped inside the doorway and looked around. The place was silent and empty. I was about to leave when I noticed the music box Rory's wizard had tracked me with had been left on the floor. I picked it up and headed back to the inn.

People began to talk excitedly and point up at the sky. Large shadows blotted out the sun and I looked up to see a plethora of white dragons flying overhead. It was Hrodin and his riders. They were flying north toward Midia. I was glad to see that he kept his word, but then bitterness swept over me as I remembered what he'd asked for in return.

Jealousy is a form of hatred, Sion said. I could feel her probing my mind but I didn't bother to shield my emotions from her.

Hrodin has no right to ask for Maren's hand, I replied. *It doesn't matter if he's truly from a royal bloodline or not.*

Do you love her?

Sion's question made me pause mid-step. Did I love Maren? It was a question I wasn't sure I had the answer to. Love was such a powerful word, and I wasn't one to cast it around fruitlessly. Maren made me feel things I didn't understand … but was that love? I didn't know.

I'm not sure, I replied. *It's confusing.*

Humans are confusing, Sion said. *Either you love her or you don't.*

It's not that easy for humans, I replied.

It is for dragons.

I didn't say anything else. A small parade of merchants passed with their carts and I could smell the delicious scents of various meats.

Are you and Demris hungry? I asked.

We found some deer earlier, Sion replied.

We're going to spend the night here. Will you two be all right by yourselves without a stable?

Yes.

Satisfied everything was set for the evening, I returned to the inn and sat in the common room for a while, listening to people talk about the latest gossip and about the coming war at the border. Once night fell, I went upstairs to get some sleep. I entered the room as quietly as possible and found Maren was asleep. I didn't want to wake her, so I laid on the floor beside the bed.

The man I'd met earlier came to mind, and I considered his tale. Was there really an island of souls somewhere? I'd have to ask Maren in the morning. It seemed likely that a sorcerer would know about such a place.

At some point, I fell asleep. I was having an odd dream about ghosts on an island when I was awakened by Maren. She was up and about and seemed her normal self again.

"Let's get moving," she said. "I'm ready to face the False King."

12

I was surprised to see how large the rider camp had grown as we began our descent. The wingless Terranese dragons were on the right side of the main camp, and Hrodin's white dragons were on the left. It was an amazing sight.

Once we landed, Maren and I walked through the camp, looking for Anesko. We didn't have to search for long. He was making his rounds and issuing orders. When he saw us, it was hard to tell what the look on his face meant.

"Master Anesko," Maren greeted. "We've just returned."

"I must say that I am both surprised and disappointed," he said. "I was surprised when the two other schools showed up. Master Katori and Master Hrodin both said you two persuaded them to come to our aid, despite the fact that the Conclave is gone. And I was disappointed that you did not return here first."

"To be fair, Councilor Flynn told me to do whatever it took to stop the False King," I said. "We were obligated to get to the other schools, especially since the magical lines of communication were destroyed. I was afraid if we came back here first, you wouldn't have let us go."

Anesko nodded. "You are correct, Eldwin. I would not have allowed you to leave. Given the situation, I would have done the same thing. I will not hold any ill favor against you, nor against you, Maren. I've called a meeting with the other masters. We need to launch an attack on the Necromancer's castle, but that beast has thwarted every attempt so far. Perhaps with the added force of riders, we can yet be successful."

"Are we attending the meeting as well?" I asked.

"No. This is for the leaders of the schools only. Once we've narrowed down our plans, we'll let the Curates inform everyone. For now, you can help the other riders prepare by gathering supplies."

Anesko headed back toward the command tent and I finally felt like a world of responsibility was no longer on my shoulders. It felt freeing. When I looked at Maren, I groaned. She had that look of mischievous curiosity that always broke the rules.

"What are you plotting?" I asked.

"Nothing bad," Maren replied. "I'm just going to listen to the meeting."

"Why? Anesko said that the Curates will tell us the plan."

"Did the last few days make you lose your sense of adventure?" She chided.

"Of course not," I said. "I just *really* liked the idea of not having to worry about anything for a moment, however brief it is."

"Well, feel free to do whatever you want. I'm

going to sneak around." She grinned and went the same direction Anesko had.

She's going to get you into trouble one day, Sion said.

I tell myself that all the time, yet I always follow after her.

Sion made a chortling sound in my mind, which I assumed was laughter. I shrugged and followed after Maren. If flying around the kingdom hadn't gotten us into trouble, I doubted listening to a meeting would. I caught up to Maren and walked beside her.

"You just can't stay away from me, can you?" She giggled.

I rolled my eyes. "You're not *that* special," I replied.

"Is that so? Hrodin seems to think so."

I glared at her. "Did you have to bring *him* up? I can't stand that barbarian lout. He makes me want to lash out irrationally."

Maren giggled again. "Sounds like you're jealous."

"Of him? No. Not even close. I'm just … protective," I replied. "Of you."

Maren grabbed my hand and quickly kissed my cheek. "I think it's cute. Don't worry about Hrodin. Once I tell my father about the arrangement, I'm sure he'll deal with Hrodin himself."

"When are you going to do that?" I asked.

"After the meeting. I haven't seen my father in months. If he doesn't already know about my time with the riders, he will today. And I'm not sure how he's going to react."

As we walked around the rear side of the command tent, Maren placed a finger over her lips, indicating I should keep quiet. I nodded and we stepped lightly to avoid making any noise.

"Are you saying I brought my men all the way here and you don't even have a plan?" Hrodin's deep voice asked.

"We are going to devise our plans together," Anesko replied. "We are from different schools and we have different ways of doing things. I want to ensure we work together as a cohesive unit rather than doing our own thing. Besides, there is a beast we must deal with before we can get close enough to the castle to attack."

"Show me this beast. Skarmundr and I will strike it from the sky," Hrodin said.

His ego was enormous.

"I wish it were that easy," Anesko replied. "In the darkness, it's almost impossible to see. We've sent a few scouts during the day and one managed to make it back to describe the creature. He said it looks like a dragon, but it appears to only be a skeleton of one. No spell or weapon the scouts attacked it with had any impact."

Maren and I exchanged glances. "A skeletal dragon?" I whispered.

Anesko continued. "The good news is, the beast doesn't cross beyond a certain boundary. We believe it's some sort of magical barrier the Necromancer has in place to keep a leash on it."

"I have heard of such a creature before." It was Katori who spoke. Her exotic accent was unmistakable.

"It is a creature of fable and I have never heard of one outside of the story, but it gives credence to your tale. The creature is called a dracolich. It is the skeleton of a dead dragon given new life through powerful dark magic. This Necromancer you mentioned, he is certainly behind it."

"Does your fable tell how to defeat it?" Anesko asked.

"Not directly," Katori replied. "The story says that the dracolich collapsed once the sorcerer was killed."

"If there is any truth to the story, then we need to kill the Necromancer to be rid of the dracolich. The problem is that we aren't able to get close enough to the castle before the beast starts devastating our forces."

"What of the king's army?" Hrodin asked.

"They are ready to march as soon as we can secure the skies," Anesko replied. "His men took heavy losses the first night we attacked, but they've since regrouped. He won't cross the border until the dracolich is dealt with."

There was silence for a moment.

"Leave the beast to me and my riders," Hrodin said. "We will keep it occupied so that the rest of you can get to the castle."

"That's suicide," Anesko said.

"What are the other options?" Hrodin asked. "My men are ready to die for glory. To live through a battle is to be respected, but to die in battle … that is the greatest honor."

"Our people are not so different," Katori said. "May we find eternal glory as we fight."

I shook my head. I had no desire to throw my life away needlessly. I would fight, yes, but I wanted to survive the battle.

"You and your men will distract the dracolich, and Katori and I will lead our forces to the castle. They have griffons, but they are easily dealt with. Once we reach the castle, we'll need to find the Necromancer quickly. I'll lead my riders into the castle to find him. Katori and her riders can keep control of the sky. Assuming this works, we'll kill the Necromancer and the dracolich dies with him."

"And if it doesn't work, we fight to the death," Hrodin said.

"I say we retreat if it doesn't work," Anesko replied. "There's no reason to die needlessly."

I mouthed the words 'thank you' to myself, glad that someone else had some common sense.

"When do we ride?" Hrodin asked.

"Within the hour," Anesko answered.

After we heard the masters leave the tent, Maren looked at me. "I need to speak with my father before we leave."

"Do you want me to come with you?" I asked.

"Yes, but I'm afraid you can't. There are some things that we must do alone, and this is one. I'll be back as soon as I can."

"I'll wait for you," I promised.

We stared into each other's eyes in silence for a moment and then Maren wrapped her arms around me and held me close. I returned her hug and breathed in the smell of her hair.

"In case something happens, I want you to know something," Maren whispered.

"Don't," I whispered back. "Whatever it is, you can tell me when this is over."

We broke our hug and Maren wiped her eyes, then rushed away. I had a feeling I knew what she was going to say, and I couldn't stand to hear the words unless I knew we had a future together. I had lost my mother and my father, and that had nearly broken me. I couldn't lose Maren, too.

I refused to.

13

"Eldwin."

I was heading to see Sion when I heard Anesko call my name. I turned to see him approaching me.

"Yes, sir?" I asked.

"We're about to fly into Midia. I know that you are technically not part of the school anymore, but you seem eager to prove yourself."

"I am," I replied.

"Good. Then I have your first mission for you."

Anesko was giving me an official task? I stood tall. "What can I do?"

"You are going to stay here," he said.

My shoulders slumped, but I didn't say anything.

"You and Sion are not battle trained, and I don't want to see either of you maimed or killed."

"I understand," I said. "It just makes me feel useless that I can't help in the battle somehow."

"You aren't useless, Eldwin. You've accomplished more than many students that have come and gone through the Citadel's doors. If Master Pevus were still alive, he would tell you the same thing."

"I will do as you ask."

"Thank you, Eldwin. When this is over, we'll talk about your place at the Citadel."

Anesko walked away, leaving me with my self-pity. I knew Sion and I weren't battle-trained, but I still wanted to help somehow. My worry for Maren's safety grew knowing that I wouldn't be out there to watch over her. Granted, she was a sorcerer and usually saved me, but still. I rescued her from Josephine, so there was that.

The time passed quickly and I stood beside Sion as the other riders flew toward Midia. In the distance, dark clouds had amassed and were beginning to blot out the sun. A storm was brewing, and I wondered how it was going to affect the battle. I'd never flown while there was a storm, but I could imagine the wind alone would be enough to cause problems for a dragon.

The wind can make it hard to fly, Sion confirmed.

My mind was completely open to the bond, and it seemed that when I didn't have my mental shield up, Sion was listening to my thoughts. I didn't mind it, but it did take some getting used to. Within minutes of the riders' departure, the storm hit the camp. Wind and rain battered the tents and forced me to seek shelter.

I ran into the first tent I saw and waited. Thunder rumbled overhead and I could see lightning flashing through the tent material. The brute force of nature was scary, but I still peeked out from the tent flaps. Some of the other tents had been knocked over or demolished completely. The cooking fires the servants had lit sputtered and sizzled as the water hit their embers. The storm seemed stronger than what was natural, and a moment later, Sion confirmed my suspicions.

This storm is fueled by magic, she told me.

The Necromancer, I replied. *He's probably trying to deter the riders.*

I can sense the dracolich, too. Its bones are crying out against its unnatural life, but the dark magic forces them to obey.

It reminded me of Esmond. He was a slave to the Necromancer's power, too. I hoped the man didn't get killed in the battle, but I knew that was a long shot.

The storm is using a lot of energy, so maybe the Necromancer will wear himself out quickly.

I hope so, I replied.

The storm did lessen after a while, but the rain continued to fall heavily. There was nothing to do other than pace around the tent. I memorized the number of steps from one side to the other, as well as from the front to the back, including the steps it took to walk around the brazier in the center. Boredom did things like that to a person.

There's someone out here, Sion said.

It's probably a servant checking on things, I replied.

Do servants sneak around with a sword?

I paused in my count of steps. *Can you see the person's face?*

No. He is wearing something over his head.

How do you know it's a man? I asked.

When bad things happen, it's always a man, Sion replied. She flashed an image of Rory's wizard standing over her, torturing her with his magic.

Fair enough, I replied. *Where is he now?*

He's near the big blue tent.

Provisions, I said. *Whoever he is, he must be looking for supplies. I'm going to check.*

I drew my blade and stepped out of the tent. The sky was still dark, but it was more like dusk than true night. I tried to walk softly, but the rain had flooded the ground and my feet squished loudly in the mud and grass. I paused outside the blue tent and readied myself, then pushed the flaps open and looked inside.

Nothing.

Well, not nothing, but there wasn't anyone inside. I released the flaps and walked around the perimeter of the tent. I saw footsteps in the mud, but there was no clear indication of the direction the person had went.

He smells familiar, Sion said.

You can smell him in the rain?

A little, she said. *It's a woodland smell.*

I heard a splashing sound, but I wasn't able to

tell where it had come from while Sion was talking to me. The rain collected on my eyebrows and sent droplets of water ran down into my eyes. I ran my index finger across them, wiping the water away. I didn't need to be blind at a time like this.

He's close, Sion said.

To me or you?

A roar answered my question and I sprinted to where Sion was. There was a figure on the ground and she had her claw on top of it.

"Don't move!" I shouted. "She'll snap your head right off."

To his credit, the man remained completely still. I stepped closer and lifted the hood of the man's face with the tip of my blade. The man looked up at me, fear in his eyes and etched onto his face.

It was Altin.

"What are you doing here?" I demanded.

"I'm sorry," Altin said. "I was trying to get away. I'll put the food back, just let me go."

"I don't care about the food," I snapped. "What are you doing in the camp?"

"I told you, I'm trying to leave. Just let me get away from here before he finds out I'm gone!"

"Who?" I asked.

"The Necromancer," Altin replied.

"Where are you going?"

"Anywhere but Midia. Please, Eldwin. I need to go!"

His tone seems genuine, Sion said.

Maybe.

"Why are you trying to leave Midia? I thought you served the False King?"

"I did, but that was before I learned the truth. I swear it!"

"What truth is that? That he's a murderer?"

"Yes! He deceived me as he has deceived many others. I don't want any part of his madness."

Let him up, I told Sion.

She removed her claw and I offered Altin my hand. He looked at it uncertainly but finally grabbed it. I pulled him up and pointed my sword at him.

"Promise you aren't lying?" I asked. "Because I would really hate to have to kill you."

"I swear on everything I hold dear," Altin said. "I overheard the Necromancer talking to Dagnis about his undead beast. He said that he was going to wipe out the dragon riders for good and no one would be able to stop him from consuming the land. That's when I realized they've been lying to me."

"Who's Dagnis?" I asked.

"The man you call the False King."

So, the mysterious man had a name. He seemed less of a danger than the Necromancer, though. At least from what I had seen so far.

"I'm sorry for leading you falsely," Altin said. "I was blind to the truth."

"Don't apologize," I said. "I know you were only doing what you thought was right. You have a good heart, Altin."

"There's something else that you should know."

"What?"

Altin looked down at the ground, avoiding my gaze. I lowered my sword and waited for him to speak.

"The man who trained you with strengthening your bond ..."

"Esmond. I know, he's a slave to the Necromancer's power."

"Yes, but his real name isn't Edmond."

"Who is he, then?" I asked.

"His name is Matthias. He's your father."

I was so startled that I dropped my sword into the mud.

"What?"

"He fell in battle and the Necromancer raised him from the grave. And that dracolich that's raising hell? It's your father's fallen dragon."

"No," I said, shaking my head. It couldn't be true. And yet, that explained why Esmond's blue eyes had seemed so familiar to me.

"I'm sorry," Altin said. "I didn't know until

after you left, or I would have said something to you. I knew that the Necromancer used his dark powers to raise the dead, but I had no idea …" he trailed off, still staring at the ground.

"Go," I told Altin. I retrieved my blade and tried to clean the mud off with my fingers. "Go and be free of the scourge that is the Necromancer. Take anything you need with you, and may you find the peace you've always wanted."

"Thank you," Altin said.

I barely heard him. I climbed up Sion's shoulder and into the saddle. There were so many emotions washing over me. Surprise, anger, pain. It was hard to sort one from the other, yet there was one thing that parted the emotions and gave me focus.

My father.

14

Sion flew through the wind and the rain, heading toward the Necromancer's castle. Down below, the stragglers of the king's army were marching in the same direction. Lightning arced through the clouds, but I didn't pay the beautiful display much attention.

I was overwhelmed with what Altin had told me. My father was alive … sort of. That was enough for me to risk my life.

And mine, Sion said.

I'm sorry, I told her. *If there is any chance at all that we can free him, we must try.*

Sion didn't reply, but I could feel her agreement through the bond. Roars of rage and pain reached my ears and it didn't take long before we were in the midst of a raging battle. Dragons and griffons fought everywhere I looked. I spotted a Terranese dragon and its rider spewing fire at two of the giant birds. Not far away, a black dragon was doing all it could to hold off a small army of griffons.

I wanted to help, but I needed to get to my father first. The wind made the rain slant at an angle and the water blinded me temporarily. Despite the powerful gusts, Sion kept herself level as she moved away from the small pockets of battle. I wiped the rain from my eyes and briefly wondered where Maren was.

Demris is near, Sion said.

Is he holding his own?

He is melting the griffons with his acid. He says Maren is fine.

I breathed a sigh of relief. Lightning lit up the sky for a few seconds and I spotted Hrodin on his massive white dragon. It looked like he was scanning the sky for something. We flew past him and continued on. The closer to the castle we got, the darker our surroundings became. I couldn't see anything on the ground.

How close are we to the castle? I asked.

A few hundred yards. I can see it ahead.

Anything we need to worry about?

I can feel magic pulsing, but I think it's the spell powering the storm.

Good, I replied. If we could get in and rescue my father while everyone else was occupied, it would greatly improve our chances of getting back to the camp without any trouble. As soon as the thought formed in my head, I caught sight of something in my peripheral. I turned to look, but there was nothing there. I knew better than to dismiss it as nothing. Reading my thoughts, Sion dived down and spun around.

Overhead, a giant shadow cut through the clouds and swooped down toward us. Another flash of lightning lit up the night long enough for me to catch a glimpse of the dracolich. It was all bone except for its wings, which had shreds of decayed flesh hanging onto them. Where a normal dragon's eyes would be, there were only red glowing orbs. Within its chest, surrounded by its ribcage, was a glowing blue sphere. It pulsed repeatedly, much like a heart.

Sion flapped her wings furiously, gaining speed and altitude as the dracolich came rushing at us. I unsheathed my blade and held onto the saddle with my good hand and waited for the dragons to slam into each other. Sion pulled back at the last second and used her rear claws to latch onto the dracolich's mid-section. I struggled to stay in the saddle and almost dropped my sword. Sion blew fire into the dracolich's face and a wave of heat filled the air around me.

I'm slipping! I cried out through the bond.

Hold on! Sion replied. She released the dracolich and pushed away, shooting through the air like an arrow. An otherworldly roar echoed across the sky and I looked over my shoulder to see the dracolich coming after us. It was much faster than I thought possible. I also didn't understand how it could fly with the state of its wings, but I guessed the magic powering its ungodly corpse was responsible.

Go faster! I urged.

I'm going as fast as I can!

Sion banked to the left, jerking me roughly to the side, then shot upward to get above the dracolich before leveling out and raking her claws along the creature's spine. Aside from scraping the dracolich's bones, Sion's attack did little damage. I leaned to the right as she flew forward and slammed my sword into the side of the dracolich's head. It had less impact than Sion's claws had.

The dracolich snapped at Sion's leg, but she ascended higher and flew in place, letting the dracolich put distance between us. The beast flipped around and opened its mouth. I expected a roar, but lightning flickered between its bony jaws before jutting out and forking in every direction. One of the bolts struck Sion and she growled in pain. I smelled something burning.

Are you all right? I shouted through the bond.

I'm fine, she replied. *It only scorched my scales.*

A green dragon came racing from the left and slammed into the dracolich. A familiar face rode on its back. Maren lifted a lance and struck the dracolich in the skull, but the beast shook its head, ripping it from her grasp.

"Maren!" I screamed.

It was too late. The dracolich's powerful jaws closed around Demris's neck and crunched down, then jerked side to side. A brief cry escaped Demris's mouth before his head lolled to the side. His massive wings stopped flapping and the dracolich released its hold. I could only watch in horrified shock as Maren and Demris plummeted toward the ground.

I was about to tell Sion to catch Maren when the

dracolich flew straight for us. Sion couldn't move fast enough, and I braced for the impact, averting my head and closing my eyes. There was a loud crash, but I didn't feel a jolt at all. I looked up to see Skarmundr had engaged the beast. Hrodin wielded his longsword and struck several powerful blows to the dracolich's skull, but it didn't faze the creature.

The dracolich broke free and slammed its bony tail into Skarmundr's side, sending the dragon reeling through the air. Sion started to dive down to race after Maren, but a griffon came in sight, heading straight for us. The sky lit up briefly and I saw my father was riding the bird. Maren was behind him, crouched and ready to leap off.

The griffon flew above us and Maren jumped, timing it perfectly. I watched her fall, her arms waving furiously before she landed on Sion's back and rolled herself forward with her momentum. The griffon banked and turned around, coming alongside Sion.

"I'm sorry!" My father, Matthias, shouted. "I'm going to make things right!"

He lifted a lance into position and the griffon sped off toward the dracolich. I wanted to tell him to stop, to come back, to flee while he had the chance. I wanted to tell him all of those things and more. Instead, I watched wordlessly as he drew closer to the undead dragon and lifted his lance, aiming for the glowing orb inside the dragon's chest.

The dracolich roared in challenge and opened its

mouth. Black flames blasted out and consumed my father and his griffon. They were scorched from existence as if they had never been there to begin with. I blinked repeatedly, thinking I must be seeing things.

But no.

They were both gone, nothing but specks of ash caught in the wind. I was too stunned to cry out. The only tangible thing that remained was the lance. It was stuck in one of the dracolich's ribs, threatening to come free. Sion read my thoughts and flew at the dracolich, blasting it with her flames as a distraction. We went underneath the creature and Maren reached up and grabbed onto the lance, jerking it free.

"That orb has to be the link to the spell!" Maren shouted from behind me. "If we pierce it, that may stop the flow of magic!"

"Nothing has hurt it!" I shouted back. "We need to get back to the camp!"

No, Sion said. *She's right. We need to stop the dracolich now.*

There was too much happening, too many thoughts and emotions clashing in my mind. I saw Hrodin and Skarmundr had recovered and the dracolich's focus was on them.

"What do we do?" I asked.

Maren didn't reply. I looked back to see her slide her palm along the tip of the lance, cutting her flesh. She dipped a finger into the blood and traced an odd symbol onto the lance's tip. The metal flared with a green light briefly. The symbol she'd traced was still there, but it wasn't wet blood anymore. It was etched into the metal.

"Get me close!" Maren shouted at Sion.

On your command, Sion told me.

Do it, I replied.

Sion turned and flew toward the undead dragon. It was engaged with Skarmundr and didn't see us approaching.

"What kind of spell did you cast?" I asked Maren, looking back again to see her face. Her expression was dark and serious.

"You'll see," she replied.

We may only get one chance at this, Sion said.

She flew under the dracolich again. Maren stood up and jabbed the lance between the dracolich's ribs. The tip of the lance flared as it struck the orb. A loud hissing sound erupted from the orb, then the lance's tip pierced the orb fully. Time seemed to still. The orb expanded and brightened in intensity, then exploded.

Maren sat back and wrapped her arms around me as we flew away from the dracolich. Sion lifted us higher into the sky and I looked down. The life fled from the dracolich's bones and the creature fell into the darkness below.

15

"It's over," I said.

"No," Maren replied. "We still need to deal with the Necromancer and the False King. I *will* avenge the death of my dragon."

I looked over my shoulder at her and could see the tears welling in her eyes. I had to turn away from her to keep from crying myself.

To the castle, I told Sion.

She looped around and I saw that all of the other riders had the same idea. Hundreds of dragons flew toward the castle, all different colors and sizes. The sight helped take my mind off my father. I could hear Maren sobbing behind me and it tore my heart into pieces. Sion and I hadn't been bonded very long, but I couldn't fathom how it would feel to lose her.

It's like death, Sion said. *That's how other dragons have described it.*

I gritted my teeth and kept my gaze ahead. So many of us had been affected in some way by everything that had happened, and it was all because of the False King. As we got closer to the castle, I could see a glowing barrier surrounding the fortress. A rider shot an arrow and the projectile exploded once it reached the barrier, much like Katori's spell had done at the Terranese school.

Another rider casted a spell at the shield. A jagged bolt of lightning arced through the air but fizzled out of existence once it hit. Three more spells were cast by others, all of them unable to penetrate the shield.

The riders want everyone with magical abilities to cast a spell at the same time, Sion told me. *They are trying to wear down the shield.*

"Do you have the energy to cast a spell?" I asked Maren without looking back at her.

"Yes, why?"

"Sion says everyone needs to cast one at that shield at the same time."

"Say when," Maren replied.

What's the signal? I asked Sion.

There's a countdown. Three. Two. One. Now!

"Now!" I shouted.

A wave of magical attacks erupted around us. Dazzling colors filled the air as fireballs, lightning bolts, and other spells filled the sky. The shield brightened in intensity as the spells hit it, but it didn't fall. The dragons joined in the attack and began blasting their breath at the shield. Flames, acid, lightning, and a multitude of spells struck the shield.

The barrier held up under the onslaught and for a moment I thought that it would be impossible to break through it, but a hole appeared in the top of the shield and it slowly spread downward until the barrier completely faded.

Griffons leaped into flight from the courtyard and began harassing the nearest dragons. Someone roared a battle cry and I scanned the sky, looking for the source. It was Hrodin. He led his riders down to the castle where they quickly dismounted and began fighting the guards who remained.

Take us down there, I told Sion.

She dove suddenly, breaking away from the other riders. Sion stopped her descent when she was only a few feet above the ground, then lifted high enough to land atop the wall surrounding the castle. Maren barely waited for Sion to fully stop before she leaped from the saddle. I followed after her, keeping my sword at the ready as we ran across the ramparts. Stone stairs led down to the courtyard and we hurried down them, taking them two at a time.

It was obvious Maren was being driven by grief and anger. I didn't blame her, but I was worried she would do something too dangerous. We reached the courtyard and I spotted the robed figure of the Necromancer. He had a glowing shield around him similar to the one that had been around the castle. Hrodin and his men were making short work of the remaining guards, easily overpowering them.

Maren stopped when she spotted the Necromancer and whispered a string of magical words. A ball of fire grew within her hands and she hurled it at him. The ball struck the Necromancer's shield and exploded, but the shield remained intact. The Necromancer turned toward Maren and glared at her. His face was nothing like I imagined. He had a youthful appearance that made me think he was the same age I was, though I assumed it was an illusion of some kind.

He lifted his left hand and pointed at Maren. I didn't see his lips move, but the air filled with whispering voices that made my skin crawl. A black ray stretched from the Necromancer's hand and struck Maren in the chest. She gasped and fell to her knees, desperately clawing at herself. I started to run towards her when a hand grabbed onto my shoulder, holding me back. I looked back and saw Katori. She shook her head and stepped ahead of me, then cast a spell of her own.

A flaming blade of magic formed in her hand and she stalked forward like a predator. She swung the blade and cut through the ray of darkness, ending the spell. Maren collapsed, her entire body shaking. Three Terranese riders rushed past me to join Katori. I hurried over to Maren and picked her up. Her body continued to tremor, making it difficult to keep her in my arms. I carried her to the stairway that led up to the ramparts and set her down.

I don't know what to do, I told Sion.

She needs to rest. It seems Katori broke the spell before it fully injured her.

I knelt beside Maren and held onto her hand while I watched Katori and her riders battle it out with the Necromancer. More riders joined us in the courtyard and added their magic to the battle, making the Necromancer sorely outnumbered. The glowing shield crackled and failed, and the Necromancer was left defenseless. Before Katori could strike him, Hrodin ran up behind him and drove his longsword through the Necromancer's back. Blood flooded from the wound, staining his robes red.

A loud cheer rang out from the other riders, but Hrodin didn't wait to bask in the adulation. He sprinted inside the castle and I knew his next target was the False King. I looked at Maren and saw that she had stopped shaking. She blinked lazily and turned her head to look at me.

"Are you all right?" I asked. My voice broke with worry.

"I'm fine," Maren whispered. "I just … need a minute."

There was a commotion as Hrodin emerged from the castle carrying his bloody sword and a human head. I assumed it was the head of the False King. He lifted his sword triumphantly and another cheer rang throughout the courtyard.

"Let's raze this cursed place!" Hrodin shouted. More cheering ensued. Maren's hand touched the side of my face, drawing my attention. She smiled weakly.

"Help me up, will you?"

I nodded and stood, then grabbed onto her hands and pulled her into a standing position. She wobbled on her feet briefly and then gained her balance, but I kept my arm around her just in case she fell. I helped her up the stairs to the rampart and pushed her up Sion's shoulder, feeling a little embarrassed with where my hands were touching her. She didn't seem to mind and climbed into the saddle. I clambered up and sat in front of her and she wrapped her arms around me.

Heat flooded my face and I could sense Sion's mirth through the bond. Sion launched herself off the wall and into the sky, circling above the castle. The other riders left the castle and the Terranese dragons began tunneling underneath it. Once they were finished, Katori and a group of riders used their magic to force the ground to collapse under the castle, destroying it. Small sections of the walls were undamaged, but the castle itself was nothing but ruins.

It could have been my imagination, but I felt like the encroaching darkness had lifted.

<h1 style="text-align:center">16</h1>

It was odd being back at the Citadel.

Sion found the stables underneath the school to be comforting and she enjoyed meeting the other dragons. Maren had spent a lot of time in her room and I had spent the last couple of days considering what my future looked like.

"As the master of the school, I have pardoned your previous expulsion and runaway," Anesko had told me. "You are more than welcome to stay here and continue to study, or you can go elsewhere if you wish. I'll leave the decision up to you, but you are always welcome here."

I'd spent a lot of time thinking about staying at the school before making my decision. There was something that had been ruminating in the back of my mind, which had been the ultimate reason behind my choice. It was foolish, I knew. And yet, if the man had been right …

I entered the north wing and made my way up the stairs to the second floor. The place held many familiar feelings and memories. I passed the room that I'd been assigned and remembered Simon. I hadn't seen him since I'd been back, and I wondered if he'd been removed after he healed. Maren's room was the last one at the end of the hall and I paused when I reached it. It was going to be difficult to leave her again, but I planned to come back. I heaved a sigh and knocked on the door.

Maren didn't answer. I waited and knocked again, but there was only silence on the other side of the door. I refused to leave before talking to her, so I tried the handle and found it unlocked.

"Maren?" I called out.

"Come in," Maren replied.

I stepped inside and closed the door behind me. Maren was sitting on her bed with her knees pulled up to her chest. She looked like she'd been crying and she was holding a crumpled parchment in her hand.

There were a hundred different ways to ask how she was feeling, but they all sounded stupid in my head, so I just sat on the edge of her bed and looked at her. She offered me a smile, but it was full of sadness.

"I'm sure everyone has been asking about me," she said.

I nodded. "Yes. Anesko said if he didn't hear from you soon, he was going to send for your father."

Maren snorted. "He could just come to check on me himself."

"Well, I think he was joking, but Anesko is always so serious, so …" I shrugged. We sat in silence for a moment, then I asked, "Are you all right?"

Maren bit her lip and shook her head.

"No, I'm not. You have no idea how this feels, Eldwin. It's like something inside me is missing, like my heart is just … gone."

"I'm sorry," I said lamely.

"It's not your fault."

"I know. I just don't know what to say," I said.

"There's nothing you can say. Just be here for me."

Those words were like a dagger plunging into my heart. Maren could read me like a book, and even though she was grieving, she still saw it on my face.

"What is it?" she asked.

I opened my mouth to reply, then paused. "I'm leaving the school," I finally said.

Maren frowned. "Why?"

"Remember when you were unconscious after burning all those griffons?"

She nodded.

"When you were resting, I ran into a man who said some crazy things. The more I think about what he said, the more my curiosity demands I find out the truth."

"What did he say?" Maren asked.

"He talked about an island where souls sometimes end up. There's a ferry that takes people to the island, but the helmsman requires a payment. The man told me that he went there looking for his wife."

"Did he find her?"

"No," I replied. "He said she wasn't there. But I've been thinking about …" I trailed off, knowing it was going to sound insane.

"Your father?" Maren asked. "Why do you think your father would be on this island?"

"I don't know. I guess because he spent the last ten years as a slave to the Necromancer? My thinking is that he's in some sort of limbo on the island."

"Let's say this island does exist," Maren said. "And let's also say that your father is on the island. What then?"

"That's the mystery," I replied. "I'm not sure if he can come back or not."

"There's a lot of unknowns with this story."

"I know, but I need to see if it's true. I can't think of anything else."

Maren regarded me in silence for a long while. I assumed she would be upset with me, but she seemed more composed than she had when I'd first come into her room. When her expression turned mischievous, I was confused.

"Do dragons have souls?" she asked.

We do, Sion said, answering the question as soon as I thought about it.

"Sion says they do."

Maren nodded.

"I'm coming with you," she said.

"You can't," I replied.

She glared at me and I raised my hands placatingly. "I'm not saying you aren't welcome to come," I said. "I'm saying you can't leave the school without Anesko's permission. The new classes are about to start, so you'd miss a lot if you weren't here."

"Since when have I ever asked permission for anything?" She asked.

When indeed? I laughed and shook my head in defeat.

"Fair enough. What about your arrangement with Hrodin?" I asked, growing serious.

Maren held out the parchment. I accepted it and uncrumpled the letter. It was from Hrodin. He'd called off the marriage. Wait.

"He changed his mind?" I asked.

"Keep reading," Maren said.

I did so and found the reason.

"'I cannot marry a dragonless rider, so our agreement is nullified.'" I handed the letter back to her.

"Talk about an insult," Maren said.

"Well, at least you don't have to go through with it now," I said.

"I know. It just stung to read that … another reminder that Demris is truly gone. I couldn't care less about Hrodin calling off the marriage."

I scooted closer to her and laid my hand on one of her knees. "I don't know how, but I think everything will be all right one day. People say time heals all wounds, and in my experience, that has tended to be true."

"Thank you, Eldwin. For everything."

"You're welcome." I patted her knee and removed my hand. "I was planning on leaving in the morning."

"That works for me," Maren replied. She leaned forward and pressed her lips to my cheek. "We go together," she said.

"Together," I replied.

THE END OF BOOK THREE

ABOUT THE AUTHOR

Richard Fierce is a fantasy and space opera author. He's been writing since childhood, but began publishing in 2007. Since then, he's written multiple novels and short stories.

In 2000, Richard won Poet of the Year for his poem *The Darkness*. He's also one of the creative brains behind the Allatoona Book Festival, a literary event in Acworth, Georgia.

A recovering retail worker, he now works in the tech industry when he's not busy writing.

He's married and has three step-daughters (pray for him), three dogs (two huskies!), three cats, two ferrets and a fish. He basically has a zoo.

His love affair with fantasy was born in high school when a friend's mother gave him a copy of *Dragons of Spring Dawning* by Margaret Weis and Tracy Hickman.

www.ingramcontent.com/pod-product-compliance
Lightning Source LLC
Chambersburg PA
CBHW032036180726
48284CB00008B/2611